A Hundred Days from Home

A Hundred Days
from Home

Randall Wright

HENRY HOLT AND COMPANY
NEW YORK

For Sarah Jane

Henry Holt and Company, LLC
Publishers since 1866
115 West 18th Street
New York, New York 10011
www.henryholt.com

Library of Congress Cataloging-in-Publication Data
Wright, Randall.
A hundred days from home / Randall Wright.
p.   cm.
Summary: After the death of his best friend, Elam reluctantly moves with his family
to the desert, where he wrestles with homesickness, loneliness, grief,
and the search for new friendship.
[1. Grief—Fiction.   2. Moving, Household—Fiction.   3. Friendship—Fiction.
4. Homesickness—Fiction.   5. Guilt—Fiction.   6. Deserts—Fiction.
7. Southwest, New—Fiction.]   I. Title.
PZ7.W95827 Hu 2002   [Fic]—dc21   2001051902

ISBN 0-8050-6885-6 / First Edition—2002
Printed in the United States of America on acid-free paper. ∞
1 3 5 7 9 10 8 6 4 2

Acknowledgments

The long journey that produced this book has taught me that successful endings do not come without support. Many people are responsible for the words that make up this story.

I would like to thank Karma for her unflagging confidence; MariD for her clear eye; and Miss Stein, my fifth grade teacher, for planting the seed. In addition there is a whole community of online friends and fellow writers who need to know how much their encouragement has meant to me.

I am grateful for an editor, Reka Simonsen, who understood what this story was about as much as I did. I am also thankful for a marvelous agent, Melanie Colbert, who believed in me and helped me believe in myself.

Lastly, though words are inadequate, I would like to thank my wonderful wife.

Oh that the desert were my dwelling-place,
With one fair spirit for my minister . . .
—Lord Byron

Chapter One

Elam stood at the top of the stairs and listened to Daddy's voice rumbling up from the kitchen. He eased down the first three steps, trying to make out the conversation.

"That's copper country," he heard Daddy say. "There's copper jobs, plenty of 'em. Jobs in the mine and jobs in the smelter."

Elam grimaced, feeling a tremor of premonition.

"But Hank," Momma answered, "that's desert country."

"Helen, I need the work . . . "

Elam leapt down the stairs, the protest ready on his lips.

" . . . and the boy needs a change."

Elam slid to a stop at the closed kitchen door, drawn up short by Daddy's all too familiar argument.

3

"Oh, Hank," Momma said. "He's doing all right. He'll be fine. He just needs time."

Elam leaned his cheek against the cool wood of the door frame. He could imagine Daddy shaking his head.

Momma's right, he pleaded silently. *I'm fine.*

"He spends too much time alone," Daddy continued. "It's not good for him. He needs a change. He needs friends."

Relaxing the frown off his face, Elam pushed through the door and let it swing shut behind him. His parents sat at the kitchen table, a battered lunchbox open between them, a steaming cup of coffee cradled in Daddy's hands.

Momma smiled. "Good morning, honey."

Daddy shifted in his chair. "Shouldn't you be off to school?"

"In a bit." Elam slumped into his seat at the end of the old oak table. "Aren't you going to work?"

"I've some business to attend to first." Daddy poured the coffee back into his thermos, closed up the lunchbox, and pushed away from the table. "I'll be home early," he said.

Elam watched him pull on his heavy coat and head out the door into the dim morning light.

That evening after supper, while they were still gathered around the table, Daddy leaned back in his chair and cleared his throat.

"I've some news," he said. "Something good for us all."

Elam glanced at Momma. She returned his gaze, her face flickering into a half-smile. She nodded at him in reassurance.

"We're leaving Springerville," Daddy announced. "I've decided to take work at the smelter in Copperton. We'll be moving as soon as school is out for the summer."

Elam examined his empty glass, turning it in the light, studying the fingerprints that smudged its sides.

"Well, what do you think?" Daddy asked.

Elam placed his glass next to his plate. "This is home," he said, staring at the tablecloth.

Daddy stood up. "Don't worry, you'll have all of springtime to say goodbye."

⸻

Later that night, Elam sat alone in the darkness of his room. He gazed out the window at the last full moon of winter rising yellow above the pines.

"Elam?" Momma peeked in through the door. "It's awful dark in here. Wouldn't you like some light?"

"I like it dark," he said.

"Well, may I come in?"

He glanced at Momma's silhouette against the brightness in the hall. "I guess."

She sat on the edge of his bed and stroked the coverlet, smoothing it down around her. "Elam, you know Daddy's just trying to do what's right for us. There's not enough work 'round here. Mr. Bowen's cutting back this spring. We're lucky your daddy had a job through the winter." She tugged at his hand. " 'Sides, the change will do us all some good."

"What about Brett?"

Momma was quiet for a minute. "You'll make some new friends," she finally said.

Elam looked out at the warm, yellow lights of the house across the road. "I don't want a new friend," he whispered.

Chapter Two

May was ending, and the Little Colorado River was swollen with the melt when Elam hiked Mount Baldy for the last time. He stood at the summit and surveyed the places he knew by heart, pointing to each with the fishing pole he carried: Big Lake, Flag Hollow, Pine Top, the Fair Grounds, the Trading Post, the Sloughs. He turned in a circle from north back to north, reaching out with the pole as if to touch each familiar site and fix it in his mind.

Once his circuit of farewells was complete, he hiked back down and hid the fishing pole behind a ponderosa pine alongside the creek where only he could find it again. After a moment's hesitation, he looked full on at the rushing water. It had been a year since he had been able to face the stream like that, especially here, at this spot. He knew he couldn't blame the river, but still it was a reminder.

He pulled a handful of leaves from a flowering sumac and threw them spiraling into the stream.

On his way home, he stopped at Flag Hollow. Purple gladiolas and blue bearded irises crowded the wrought-iron fence, pushing up through a riot of new spring growth. He ran his hand across the familiar headstone and traced out the carving: *Brett McClellan, born January 13, 1949; died May 12, 1960.*

He lingered for another moment, then meandered back home, arriving just in time to tell it goodbye, too.

Chapter Three

A day later, Elam sat alone beneath a thinly leafed chinaberry tree. He pulled at the thorn plants that grew in their new yard, but the baked ground held them fast. He shifted his seat. The warmth had burned through his jeans, near blistering his backside, so he squatted on his heels and pulled at another of the sprawling plants. It broke off at the root.

He got up to stretch out his legs and to take a look at his new surroundings.

Their house stood on the butt-end of a ridge—an arid hogback that rose up in a wide ripple from the desert floor. At the far end of the ridge, through a shimmering haze, Elam could make out the copper smelter. Its smokestack pierced the faded sky. Between them ranged the long row of company houses, built from brick and clapboard and roofed with tin. Halfway to the smelter a massive trestle bridge spanned the front canyon connecting Smelter Road with town.

His house, like all the other homes on the ridge, had been raised up from the level of the street, the yard filled in and held in place by a cinderblock retaining wall—as if the desert earth had been too hard for the construction. A less forbidding soil had been hauled in, providing the house with room for a cellar and a patch of yard.

All that grew in the yard now were dry clumps of grass and the obstinate thorns that broke off at the root—and the chinaberry tree and a giant cottonwood in the back yard. The trees offered only a thin shade against the midday heat.

Elam gazed up into a cloudless sky and thought how much he would have enjoyed such a day back home, up in the mountains—a day of blues and greens and pleasant warmth, accompanied by the sweet smells of balsam and pine, and the sound of water tumbling through a meadow.

But here, there was no pleasure in the sun-bleached air.

He wiped his forehead on his sleeve and went back inside.

Momma had just pulled a china cup from a

packing box. "You put all your things away yet?" she asked.

Elam blinked, trying to adjust his eyes from the brightness outside. "Can't I just leave it in the boxes?"

With a grunt, Daddy came in through the kitchen door followed by Uncle Jack, Daddy's oldest brother. He had come down to help them with the move. Between them, they wrestled Momma's stuffed chair through the door.

"Where you want this?" Daddy asked.

Momma glanced around the room. "By the window there."

They settled the chair into place. "That's everything," Daddy said.

"Does that mean I can get back to home now?" Uncle Jack asked, wiping his forehead with a handkerchief. "Whew! But it's hot." He flopped into the chair.

"It's going to get hotter," Momma said. She turned to Elam. "And no, you can't just leave your things in the boxes."

Elam groaned at her, then slouched off to his room. He had already assembled his bed in the far corner. The chest of drawers containing his clothes and other valuable possessions stood against the wall, just under the only window. Several cardboard boxes sat on the floor. He opened the first box and quickly glanced through its contents—old photographs and assorted odds and ends not worth unpacking—except for a single, tattered picture. He lifted out the photograph and placed it in the top drawer of his dresser, behind his tee shirts, next to an old tobacco tin. With a grunt, he shoved the full box into a corner of the closet. He then turned to the remaining boxes. Once unpacked, he carried them outside to the cellar door, where Momma had been stacking the rest of the empties.

Now that his things were all stowed away, Elam explored the house, peering into rooms that contained familiar belongings made strange by their new surroundings. It was a small house, but in the dim light of shaded windows and unfamiliarity it seemed huge to Elam. It smelled musty and close, as if its air had not been breathed in ages. At least it was less forbidding than the air outside.

"Mom," he called.

"I'm in here," she answered from her bedroom. She was refolding Daddy's workpants and laying them neatly on shelves in the closet.

"Your father and Uncle Jack have gone up to the smelter to let them know we're all moved in," she said.

Elam leaned against the wall. "It's like an oven out there."

Momma laughed. "Well, at least we'll save money on gas."

"Huh?"

"When I bake cookies, I'll just set them out the window for a few minutes, and they'll be done."

"They'll burn up," Elam said.

A few hours later Elam watched Uncle Jack drive away in his pickup, heading back to Springerville and its cool evening air. Elam wished he could go with him.

Chapter Four

Early on the first Monday of June, Elam followed his father out the front door of their new house and let the screen door bang shut behind him. He squinted in the bright light of morning.

"What'll you be doing up there?" he asked.

Daddy paused on the walk. "Whatever they need. Whatever they ask me to do." He snorted a laugh. "Mostly shoveling, I expect." He adjusted the old, battered lunchbox he carried under his arm. "There's boys your age just up the road. You should get along and introduce yourself."

"Maybe. If Momma doesn't need my help."

Daddy nodded and stepped down through the gate. Elam shifted his bare feet on the walk. Not yet seven o'clock and the cement was already getting too warm.

Later on, in the broad heat of noon, Elam stood in the back yard in his tennis shoes and stared across the canyon to the far ridge—at the dusty outline of cactus and mesquite. Above him the cottonwood leaves rustled, though he could feel no breeze. He let his gaze wander the length of the canyon. He imagined he could make out the remains of a dried-up watercourse along the canyon floor. He sniffed the air, hoping for the smell of moss and willow, but instead the heat sucked his nostrils dry and made his throat itch. He ducked in through the screen door and filled a glass from the kitchen sink.

"There's cold water in the icebox," his mother said.

But he drank the tepid water he had already drawn, swallowing it in three gulps. He smacked his tongue at the salty aftertaste.

"It looks like there's a river in the canyon," he said.

"It's just a dry wash," his mother answered. "I expect there's only water when it storms. You stay up out of there when it's raining. It could wash you clean away."

Elam found the idea absurd. "The day it rains here, I'm goin' fishing."

Momma laughed. "I'd bet there's not a fish for a hundred miles."

———————————

After dinner Elam sat on his bed in the dusky half-light of his room, staring at the tattered photograph — a school picture of a skinny, towheaded boy, grinning so his eyes sparkled. Elam ran a finger over the picture's dog-eared corners. Except for Elam's brown hair, Momma'd said they could have been twins. Elam had always wished they were.

He flipped the photo over and back, over and back, turning it in his hands so that the face and the faded blue ink of the inscription blurred in his eyes. He knew the inscription by heart: *To my friend Elam, from your friend Brett.*

A sudden knock on his door made him clamp the picture tight between his palms.

"Son?"

The door squeaked open and Daddy poked his head into the shadowed room. "Need some light?" He flipped on the switch without waiting for an answer.

Elam squinted in the sudden brilliance.

Daddy stepped through the open door. "How are you liking it here?" he asked.

Elam shrugged.

"You ought to get out and make some friends."

Elam shrugged again. "There was too much to do today," he said.

"Well, tomorrow then." Daddy eased back out the door, shutting it behind him.

Elam unclasped the photograph.

"I don't like it here at all," he whispered to the picture.

Chapter Five

After Brett died, Elam discovered that he liked being alone in the mountains, hiking through the ponderosa pines, exploring the crags and canyons and grassy meadows. It made him feel big as the trees—like he was part of the mountains themselves. When he was alone like that, he could feel as if Brett were still with him.

But today, when he stepped across the back road toward the desert canyon, he shrank inside. He felt out of place among the strange noises that buzzed and snapped through the dry air.

He carefully made his way down the near slope. Bizarre plants and shrubs scattered the hillside: emerald-skinned trees with miniature leaves and thorny branches; dark green bushes that gave off a pungent aroma that reminded Elam of freshly oiled railroad ties; cacti of assorted shapes and sizes from tiny pincushions to giant armed sentinels. He peered intently into the shadows beneath the strange plants, wondering what kind of life they might harbor. From the corner of his eye he thought he caught a movement, but when he turned to look there was no sign that anything on the hillside had ever changed.

"Is someone there?"

He frowned at the harsh sound of his own voice—an intrusion that was quickly swallowed by the blistering air.

He skirted a bristling, segmented cactus that was nearly as tall as he was. He picked his way through a prickly pear that sprawled in haphazard lethargy across the ground. He stopped and glanced at the faded sky. His vision darkened for an instant, folding in from the sides. His heart fluttered. Then the day returned to normal.

He ran back up to the house, into its shaded kitchen, and poured a glass of water from the pitcher in the icebox.

His mother was just sweeping breakfast crumbs out from under the table.

"Momma," he said. "Do you think there's ghosts here?"

She stopped with the broom raised just off the floor. "What?"

"I do. I think there's ghosts here."

"Whatever makes you say that?"

Elam sipped at the cold water. It still left a brackish aftertaste in his mouth. "Can't you feel 'em when you go outside?"

She shook her head. "When I go outside," she said, "I just feel hot."

Chapter Six

Today, with a canteen strapped to his waist and a walking stick clutched in his hand, Elam set out to explore the back canyon. It was still early. Breakfast was put away and Daddy had just left for work. The desert seemed quieter at this hour and the morning air more at ease.

He hiked across the broad slope to where it fell away to the canyon floor. From there he found a shoulder of gray earth and rock that eased down to the valley's bottom. As he descended, kicking up clouds of dust, the sun climbed, and soon the bushes and cacti themselves seemed to accompany him with their own mysterious clickings and whisperings.

He paused on the bank of the dry wash. It was like a river of sand that flowed through the center of the canyon, confined within overhanging ledges of hard-baked earth. He sat on the bank and dangled his feet in the arid stream, stirring up the sand with the toe of a tennis shoe. He jumped down and began to dig with his hands. Within half a foot the sand turned damp. He scraped frantically at it, thinking that maybe if he dug deep enough, the hole would fill with water. By the time it was elbow deep, the handfuls of sand he scooped out were still only damp.

He slumped back and brushed the grit off his shirt, then took a long drink from his canteen. After a quick glance at the sky, he poured the remaining water into the hole he had dug. He stopped to listen. With the canteen still suspended before him he looked about. Had he imagined that deep sigh of contented relief?

He scrambled up the hillside to his house on the end of the ridge.

"Momma," he called as he pushed through the back screen door. He pulled up short when he realized she wasn't alone. Another woman sat at the kitchen table with her.

"Elam," Momma said, "this is our neighbor Rhea—Mrs. Gardner. I invited her over for a visit."

Mrs. Gardner smiled. She looked to be about Momma's age. "Hello, Elam."

Elam nodded a hasty greeting. With a final glance out the back door, he retreated to his room.

Chapter Seven

"Momma," Elam said the next afternoon just after lunch. "Why'd we have to come here?"

His mother folded her arms and leaned back against the kitchen counter. "Already?"

Elam turned to her with a puzzled look. "Already what?"

She smiled. "Barely here a week and already wanting to go back?"

He looked at the floor, embarrassed that she could guess so easily what he was thinking. "I didn't say that."

"You didn't need to, the way you've been moping around here. You just need to get out and make some friends is all."

"Well, couldn't we just go back for a couple of days?"

"Your daddy'll be working the swing shift come Saturday. He won't be able to take the time."

"When can he?"

"You'll have to ask."

At ten to three Elam ran out to watch for his father. He stood in the front road and shifted from foot to foot, staring toward the smelter at the far end of the ridge. After a bit he let his gaze wander across the front canyon toward town. Houses lined that hillside, too, their back yards spilling into the tumbled rock and cottonwood of the canyon. Down below there really was a river of sorts—a chemical stream that flowed from the smelter, meandering through green stands of poplar and scrubby pomegranate. From where Elam stood he could detect the faint odor of sulfur.

A shrill whistle from the smelter announced the shift change. He stood on his tiptoes to get a better view down the road, but it was another ten minutes of waiting before he spied his father in the distance, his white hardhat glimmering in the sunlight. Elam dashed forward to meet him.

"Dad," he said, speaking between gasps for breath. "Mom says maybe we can go back home for a visit."

Daddy took off the hardhat and wiped his arm across his forehead. "She did, huh?"

Elam nodded.

"Well, maybe in August, after I've earned a couple of vacation days."

He put his arm around Elam and steered him toward home. At the top of the steps on the cement walk, Daddy suddenly knelt down. "Son, come here."

Elam squatted by his side. "What?"

"Listen." His father spat on the cement. "Can you hear it sizzle?"

Elam nodded.

Daddy stood up and chuckled. "By August I bet it evaporates before it even hits the ground."

Elam frowned. It was already too hot to bear.

Chapter Eight

On Friday Elam awoke in the dark to mournful wailings. A yipping and howling filled the early air with phantom harmonies that sounded as if they were right outside his window.

He pulled a blanket over his head, but the muffled voices turned eerier still. His breathing felt thin and unnatural under the covers, so he climbed out of bed and hurried toward the glow of light from the kitchen. There he found his father hunched over a cup of steaming coffee.

"What gets you out of bed so early?" Daddy asked.

"What's that noise?"

"Coyotes. Must be chasing around down in the back canyon. Kind of spooky sounding, ain't they?"

Elam nodded and sat across from his father.

"I thought they might be ghosts," he said.

"They're that, too. They'll keen up a storm, but you'll never see 'em."

As the sun crept over the distant hills, the howling trailed off into nearly nothing, replaced by the peaceful *croo-croo* of the mourning doves.

———

Later, after lunch, Elam stood at the very edge of the back road and peered into the canyon, searching for any trace of the coyotes. He examined the near slope. He scanned the canyon's length. At this hour everything was still. The only movement was the shimmer of midday heat flowing along the sandy wash. The only sounds were faint whisperings as the heat rose from the desert floor. Elam stepped once again into the canyon.

At its bottom, he knelt and traced his finger across the burning sand. "They can't be ghosts after all," he said.

Animal tracks crisscrossed the dry wash. Elam squatted to examine them closely, but it was impossible to pick a single trail out of all the confused traces. He rose and hunted along the far bank, keeping alert for strange sounds or unexpected movement. Finally he discovered prints in the sand of a dry gully that emptied into the wash. He followed the track, ducking into the shade of an overhanging palo verde.

The gully had been carved over time by cascading water that had washed a series of steps out of the hillside, exposing the rocks and grit-hardened clay beneath. Elam climbed upward, keeping to the gully, and soon came to a spot where it widened out to form a small basin. He wiped the sweat off his face and forehead with the front of his tee shirt, then took off the shirt and wrapped it around his head like a turban.

A large mesquite tree grew on the hillside near the edge of the basin, shading a portion of its sandy floor. Elam slumped into the shade and leaned back against the rough dirt wall beneath the tree. His tongue had become thick in his mouth and his lips felt rough and dry. He yearned for a sip of water.

A rustling from above made his breath catch. The noise turned into a clicking purr. He peered over the bank. A forked tongue flitted just inches from his nose.

Elam froze. He felt as if everything had drained to a pit in his stomach. Darkness flickered at the edges of his vision. The coiled diamondback was the largest he had ever seen, nearly as thick as his leg. Its angular head weaved from side to side as it sampled the air with its tongue.

The snake rose up, and Elam snapped his eyes closed, afraid it would strike at his face. The rattling clicked to a halt. Elam waited, wondering if it had crawled away. After a moment he peeked through narrowed eyelids. The rattler was still there, its neck stretched two feet into the air, its head held rigid.

Elam tried to swallow the dryness out of his throat. The snake rose higher. Elam eased back. The rattler stretched further up.

With his eyes fixed on the snake, Elam crawled to his feet. The diamondback reached higher still, but it couldn't sustain the height. It fell to its side and after a brief squirming, slithered into the brush.

Elam's vision lightened as if the sun shone just a little brighter, burning down through the shade of the mesquite.

━━━━━━━━━━━━━━

That evening Elam sat beneath the yellow light of the kitchen with his father and mother. Dinner was over and the table cleared.

Daddy pulled at his shirt collar. "I ought to climb up on the roof and get that cooler fixed. It's getting mighty warm."

Momma sipped her iced tea, and then held the glass to her cheek. "It would make the days a bit more bearable."

"I saw a diamondback today," Elam said. "It was a big one."

Daddy sat up in his chair. "Where?"

"Down in the canyon."

"You weren't out there by yourself, were you?"

Elam shrugged. "Why not? I never had any trouble back home."

"This isn't home," Daddy said. "You've gotta be careful. Things are different here. If you're gonna be tramping around out in the desert, you've gotta take somebody with you."

Momma set down her glass. "Elam, your daddy's right. You have a lot to learn about this country."

"It was just a snake," Elam said. "We've got rattlers back home. Besides, I think this one was tame."

"Tame?" Momma asked.

"Yeah. At first it rattled at me. But then it did something strange."

Daddy frowned. "It struck at you? Elam, you've got to—"

"No, it just kind of reared up, like it was trying to stand."

Daddy looked puzzled. "Really?"

"Yes, but then it fell over and crawled away."

"It just crawled away? It didn't try to bite you?"

"Nuh-uh. It didn't strike at all."

Daddy shook his head. "Hmmph. That's how rattlers fight with each other, how they show their strength. The one that can rise up the highest is the king."

Elam pushed his chair back from the table and stood up. "I guess that makes me the king then!"

Chapter Nine

Elam dreamed of snakes all that night. He dreamed of tawny coils of desert sand that rose up with flickering tongues to pay him honor. And he dreamed of water, flowing over desert rocks, spreading the arid landscape with a teeming life.

When he awoke to morning, his left hand felt thick and clumsy, and when he looked in the bathroom mirror, he could see red fingerprints etched on his cheek. As he leaned on the sink, pinpricks of renewed circulation began to tingle in his hand. He shook it to relieve the burning sensation.

A cotton-like dryness filled his mouth. He ducked his head under the tap and rinsed his hair in the lukewarm stream. Then he drank his fill.

As he gazed at his dripping face, he felt a thrill at

the memory of the snake. And he shivered when he remembered his father's words: *the highest is the king.* What would it mean to be king of the snakes?

"Elam," his mother called, interrupting his musing. "Breakfast."

He rubbed his hair dry with a towel and took another look at himself in the mirror. It seemed he could see a double reflection, a faint duplicate of himself, just beyond his regular image.

"Coming," he yelled back to his mother.

The clock over the stove showed seven-ten.

"Daddy gone to work already?" Elam asked as he sat at the table.

"You slept in," Momma said.

Elam poured a bowl of dry cereal. "I was dreaming about that snake."

Momma clucked her tongue.

Elam shoved a spoonful of cornflakes into his mouth. "Did you know Brett almost got bit by a rattler once?"

"Elam! Don't talk with your mouth full."

He swallowed. "Out in Pierce's field. Down by the willows. A big one."

Momma nodded. "I know."

"But not as big as the one I saw yesterday."

"Honey, you stay away from them. I think your daddy's right. You shouldn't be wandering around out there alone." She mussed his hair, interrupting his protest. "I know, I know. You were king of the mountains back home. But you had Brett."

"If we were still home, I wouldn't need anybody."

Momma picked up the laundry basket she had set on the table. "Well, you should get out and make friends here anyway. Mrs. Richards has three sons. One of them is just your age. And the Heights have a boy, too. You should go introduce yourself."

Elam shrugged his shoulders and shoved another spoonful of cereal into his mouth. "Maybe," he mumbled.

When Elam finally left the house that morning, he stood at the edge of the dirt road and searched the canyon for the gully he had climbed the day before. With a hand shading his eyes, he wondered if the dark smudge against the hillside was the mesquite where he had found the diamondback.

He trudged along the dusty road. A lizard scurried across his path and up the cinderblock retaining wall that bounded the neighbor's yard. The lizard paused at the top, cocked up like a spring, then shot off along the wall and disappeared into the shade of an oleander bush that grew in the yard.

Elam zigzagged as he walked, meandering toward the Richardses' house—the big white house, Momma had said, with the pomegranate trees in the back yard.

He found the house and passed it by, heading on to the Heights'—three houses down and next to the company-owned tennis court. Daddy said they called it the cement court and that it didn't look fit for tennis anymore.

He heard voices and ducked behind the Heights' back wall. Quietly he inched his way forward. At the corner he peered around the cinderblocks.

A group of five or six boys huddled in the center of the tennis court. A match flared, and they all backed away, leaving a lizard to squirm on the cement, sparks shooting from its mouth.

Elam jumped at the loud bang.

The clap of the explosion bounced off the far hillside. Elam could smell burned gunpowder. The lizard had vanished. A split second later the group of boys erupted with laughter.

"Did you see that?" one said. "Blew it to pieces."

"Nothin' left," said another.

Elam pulled back behind the wall in disgust, but he tensed himself when he heard a voice coming closer.

"I'm gonna get me another one," the voice said.

Elam ran back the way he had come, then he dashed across the road and ducked behind a large creosote bush.

He peeked through its branches.

A tall, sandy-haired boy stood in the road staring at him. "Hey, who are you? You that new kid?"

Elam backed out of the bush, spun around, and raced down the hillside into the canyon. When he hit the wash he turned right and hurried on.

He slowed as he approached the gully he had climbed yesterday. With the back of his hand, he wiped the sweat off his face. His fingers still carried the thick, pungent odor of creosote.

He glanced back. No one had followed. He dropped to his knees in the sand.

"I want to go home," he whispered.

He looked up at the rising hillside. "I hate it here!"

The sand was hot on his knees.

"I want to go home!"

Finally he couldn't bear the heat any longer. He jumped to his feet and kicked at the sand, sending up a shower that got into his eyes and mouth. Spitting and sputtering, he ran to the edge of the wash and snatched up a rock.

"Can't you just let me be!"

He threw the rock at the hillside and hit a bristling cactus, sending thorny segments flying. He picked up another rock and bounced it off the side of a giant saguaro that stood back away from the wash.

He grabbed another rock and took aim at the palo verde that overhung the gully.

"I want to go—"

He stopped with his arm cocked. A thin, dog-like creature stood in the shade of the tree, its head lowered between splayed front legs.

"A coyote!" Elam cried.

The animal spun about and raced away.

Elam dropped the rock and chased after the coyote, scurrying beneath the palo verde, up through the gully, and on through the first sandy basin where he had seen the snake. On his hands and knees he climbed up the next series of rocky steps, finally emerging into a deep alcove that had been carved into the hillside by aeons of desert rain. There he had to stop. The wall before him was too steep and high to continue. But that was not what had brought him to a halt.

He stared, openmouthed, at the delicate green plant that had taken root there in the relative cool of this natural basin.

It was the sapling of a mountain pine.

Chapter Ten

Elam left home in the early hours, with the pale light of dawn just creeping into the sky. He moved slowly so that he didn't spill the bucket. Navigating the hillside with the heavy pail was more difficult than he had anticipated. He kept surging ahead of himself, nearly stumbling over his own feet. And each time he lurched to a stop, water splashed out of the bucket, onto his shoes, and into the dry earth, where it quickly disappeared.

By the time he reached the bottom of the canyon his feet were soaked and the bucket was nearly half empty. He crossed the wash and lugged the bucket up the gully, hauling it over each rocky step. When he reached the sheltered basin, he dribbled the remaining water around the sapling, spooning it out with his hand, careful not to wash the soil away from its roots.

He returned home, the empty bucket rattling in his grasp. He paused at the back door and peeked in. He had heard laughter from inside. Mrs. Gardner was there, sitting with Momma. The two women talked and laughed as if they had known each other forever.

Elam crept around the house and quietly let himself in through the front door.

Chapter Eleven

Daddy was on swing shift at the smelter. He worked from three in the afternoon until eleven at night, leaving Elam and Momma alone through the warm evenings. After work Daddy walked home along the dark row of company houses, following the road from one end of the ridge to their house on the other. Momma would leave a covered plate of dinner out for him. By morning the plate was always clean and put away.

Despite Daddy's late hours, when Elam dragged himself out of bed just before sunrise one early morning, a light was already shining in the kitchen and the smell of coffee percolated through the house.

Daddy sat at the kitchen table.

"Up early again?" he asked.

Elam yawned and rubbed his eyes.

"Seem to be making a regular habit of it," Daddy said. "Where you been going off to?"

Elam slumped into a chair and pretended he didn't hear, not wanting any more lectures from his father about the dangers of the desert.

"Well?" Daddy took a sip from his cup as he waited for an answer.

"Making friends," Elam said, hoping that would satisfy him.

"Oh? With who? Dicky Height? Mike Richards?"

Elam stared at the tabletop. "Yeah."

He heard the chink of the cup as Daddy set it down.

"No you haven't. I work with their dads. They say their boys have never even talked to you."

Elam kept his eyes fixed on the tabletop, searching its oak-grained pattern. He was getting tired of Daddy's smothering concern.

"Son, you've got to come out of yourself. You can't just—"

Suddenly Elam jerked his head up. "Why not?" he shouted. "Why can't I?"

He pushed away from the table and slammed through the back screen door, letting it bounce an echo across the canyon.

He winced as a ray from the rising sun slipped over the horizon and flashed into his eyes. He grabbed the empty pail and filled it at the faucet under the kitchen window, ignoring Daddy brooding at him through the screen door.

With the bucket full, he headed into the canyon and up the other side toward the hidden basin, to that tiny tree that seemed to have come all the way from his mountain home just to keep him company.

After eight days, two trips a day, his balance and strength had improved. Very little water had spilled by the time he eased into the sheltered alcove.

He stepped across the cool sand, and a touch of moisture brushed across his face. He gazed in wonder at the sheen of water that rippled over the wall before him, trickling down to darken the sand around the sapling. He reached out and touched the rocky face. His fingers glistened as he pulled them away. He touched them to his lips.

Stepping back, he gazed up at the water that oozed over the curved rim above. He lowered his bucket to the sand and retreated from the shaded alcove.

With the rising sun in his eyes, he climbed out of the gully to the left and up the steep hillside, skirting the sheer sides of the basin. Rocks and dirt slid down behind him. He clutched at desert sage and wire grass as he scrambled up the slope. Avoiding the dangerous cliff face took him further out and higher than he had anticipated. Sweating and gasping, he circled around and finally came upon the gully again, much higher up the hill. He paused to rest, pulling his shirt away from his sticky skin.

Here the gully was shallower and wider—an open swath where the thin layer of dirt had washed away to expose the hard-baked rock and clay beneath. In order to reach the rim of the basin and the cascading stream, Elam now had to follow the dry bed downward. With the sun scorching the back of his head and neck, he began to wonder if maybe he had imagined the water. It didn't seem possible that such a stream could survive even the early morning heat. A cicada zapped and clicked from the bushes off to his right.

The gully began to narrow where it had eaten deeper into the hillside. It formed a series of steps where the softer, sandy layers had given way to desert storms, and the more resistant, time-hardened strata were left standing as ledges within the stream.

Elam hiked downward. He heard it before he saw it—the unmistakable gurgling of water bubbling up from the ground. He breathed a sigh of relief that it hadn't been his imagination after all.

At the foot of the last step, just at the edge of the fall into the sapling's basin, a spring of water welled up from the ground, forming a small pool that overflowed to cascade down the wall.

Elam dropped to his knees and splashed his hot face. He shivered as the water trickled down his neck and back. Leaning against the step behind him, he relished the feel of moisture in the air.

He had heard of desert springs before—artesian wells that bubbled up from the depths beyond the reach of the desert sun. Perhaps this one had remained inactive until just this day, lying dormant until it was time to come alive to water the sapling below.

Elam lay on his side in the cool sand by the pool and rested from his climb. He closed his eyes and let the gurgling sounds send his mind back to times before, when he had napped amongst the pine trees at a rushing river's edge. His thoughts lost their focus, becoming blurred by the cool comfort he felt. He heard a voice calling to him across the tumbling water. Brett, calling through the shimmering water that cascaded over his shadowy form and dampened the sapling at his feet. Brett, calling for Elam to wake up and take him home.

Elam opened his eyes. The voice continued from somewhere down below, way off in the canyon. Two voices, shouting and laughing. Then others.

The hike to the canyon floor proved to be more difficult than the climb had been. Elam slipped and slid through the brush, scraping his hands and elbows, bruising his backside and legs. But still he hurried, running straight down the hillside now, anxious to find whoever had been calling to him.

He slowed as he neared the bottom of the canyon. The voices were no longer shouting, but he caught snatches of conversation and an occasional explosion of laughter.

They had not been calling him after all.

He ducked into the gully that he had climbed up from the wash, keeping himself hidden beneath its bank as he continued his descent. He reached the shade of the palo verde and peered out.

A group of boys lay sprawled in the sand while a single boy knelt in the center of the wash, fiddling with a large, rusty object.

"You got that thing set yet?" another boy asked.

"Hey, you wanna do it?" the first one replied. He grunted a couple of times and then said, "There! It's done."

He placed the object on the sand. Elam recognized it—an animal trap. He had seen one before, in the forest near home. That one had been sprung, with the chewed-off leg of some animal still in it.

"Okay, ready for the bait," said the first boy. "Come on, Dicky, give it here."

Another boy tossed him a white paper package.

"You really think bologna will work?" Dicky asked.

"Don't see why not. My dog loves bologna. Coyotes should like it fine, too."

"Yeah, but your dog's a wiener dog."

The first boy threw a handful of sand at Dicky. "You're a wiener."

Elam shook his head at the noise—after being alone all morning, the babble grated on his senses. He shrank down beneath the bank and waited for the boys to leave.

It wasn't long before their chattering began to fade away. Elam peeked over the bank. The raucous group was scrambling up the far hillside and out of the canyon.

Once the boys disappeared beyond the curve of the upward slope, Elam jumped into the wash. With a toe, he eased the bologna-bait away from the hidden trap. He kicked at the sand, clearing it away to expose jagged jaws that formed a circle of teeth around the paddle-shaped trigger. This trap was meant for an animal much larger than a coyote. Elam searched about for a stick or branch, ranging away from the wash to find a tool strong enough for his purpose. He finally settled on an arm-length rib section of a decayed saguaro cactus that had long ago fallen to its death.

With his chosen tool he pushed at the trigger mechanism to spring the trap. It snapped shut, splintering the saguaro rib and stinging Elam's hands with its force. He dropped the rib to shake the pain out of his fingers.

A flash of movement down the wash a pace caught his eye. He spun about, his heart jumping into his throat. A coyote stood in the middle of the wash, staring back at him.

For a full minute Elam kept himself still, his gaze fixed on the animal. Then cautiously he bent down to pick up the bologna. The coyote lowered its head. With a quick motion, Elam flung the meat toward the animal. The coyote jerked back, startled. But then it stepped forward, nosing at the bait with its sharp snout. After making sure of the scent, it snatched up the bologna, sprang away down the wash, and darted into the brush that edged the bank.

Chapter Twelve

The coyote wailing that awoke Elam seemed to come from a single animal. And from a distance. A lonesome howling that eased through Elam's consciousness to rouse him out of a quiet dream of rushing water. He awoke to darkness and the echo of the trailing cry. He sat up and listened. The house was silent. He slid out of bed and padded through the dark kitchen to the back door. The door itself had been left open, leaving the screen as the only defense against the night.

Another mournful cry carried across the canyon, making Elam shiver, though the outside air was warm on his skin.

He hurried back to his room, pulled on a pair of jeans, and quick-laced his tennis shoes. Then he slipped through the screen door and eased it closed behind him.

Without the sun searing the sky, the nighttime warmth was comfortable against his skin. Elam became conscious at once of smells that in the broad light of day were thin and scattered: the dark pungency of the creosote and mesquite; the cloying cactus blossoms that had found their springtime this late in the year. And with them came the hint of another scent that was out of place in this desert world—the distant smell of water on willows.

The setting moon lit Elam's descent into the canyon. The moon was several days past full, but still it shone brightly in the desert air, illuminating the hillside with its reflected light.

In addition to the smells, Elam also became aware of noises that were absent in the daytime: animal-like scrabbling in the underbrush; squeakings as bats flitted about, devouring the insects that, too, were on the wing; the hooting of an owl. And then once more the keening wail of the coyote.

He shivered again and glanced up at the far ridge, expecting to see a silhouetted form arched back against the night sky, but only the giant saguaros broke the boundary between earth and stars.

He looked about. In the darkness the desert

seemed less brooding and oppressive—the daytime ghosts were quiet, and that surprised him. The usual fear of the dark had melted away in the recognizable rustlings and rootings of the night creatures. But for the strange shapes of the trees and cactus he might be back home.

He picked his way down the slope under the dwindling light of the moon. By the time he reached the wash at the bottom, the moon had slipped beyond the hill behind him. The sky above the opposite ridge turned a deep, velvety blue. He paused and listened, hoping to hear the coyote once again. He waited, scanning the hillside, which remained in shadow. The coyote kept its silence.

Elam climbed toward the sapling, following the familiar gully up through the darkness. Already he could hear the tinkle of the cascading spring. He sniffed the air. The smell of water was unmistakable. He hurried on. When he finally entered the sheltered alcove, he felt he should bow his head.

In the darkness the sapling appeared larger than he remembered. A pool of water had formed about it, reflecting the fading stars overhead. The pine tree rose up from an island within that mirrored sky.

Elam could feel a smile spread across his face. It seemed silly to be grinning all alone in the darkness, so he tried to stifle the smile. But it returned against his will. He gave up the fight and sank down on the sand at the edge of the basin, happier than he could remember being for a long while.

The sand on which he sat was damp, but he remained there and watched the shimmering reflections in the pool, hoping to prolong his joy until the desert daytime came to burn the magic out of this place.

When Elam awoke, the alcove was still in shadow—a daytime shadow now that had replaced the mystical darkness of the night. He yawned and stretched. His tee shirt was damp, making his back itch. He climbed to his feet and brushed the sand from his jeans. He yawned again and rubbed the sleep from his eyes. Then he stopped in surprise.

The pool of water surrounding the pine sapling had not been a nighttime fancy. Streamers of moss undulated at its edges. And in the center of the pool, on a sandy mound, stood the tree, almost three feet tall.

Water rippled as it cascaded down the alcove wall, filling the pool. It wouldn't be long before it overflowed this basin and found its way down the gully, into the dry wash.

Elam started at the sound of pebbles rattling down from above.

"The coyote," he whispered.

He spun about, sprinted out of the basin, and headed up the hillside. Over the last few days, he had explored around the gully and found a rough trail that led off to the right. It angled across the slope and back again, leading almost directly to the spring above. He raced up the trail, keeping as quiet as he was able in his effort to head off the animal before it escaped.

As he neared the upper pool he slowed, keeping low to the ground. He paused behind a clump of ragged bushes. A noise of movement came from just beyond—a scraping and clattering sound, like hard-soled shoes treading on rock.

Elam peeked out. A scrawny, black-haired boy stood at the edge of the small pool with his back to Elam. The boy wore canvas pants tucked into scuffed cowboy boots and a white tee shirt, which emphasized the deep brown of his arms and neck.

Elam felt his heart sink at the realization that his secret place had been discovered.

He ducked behind the bushes, for the black-haired boy had turned to scan the ridge above. Peering through the scraggly growth, Elam scrutinized the brown profile, noting the dark eyes and soft features. He crouched low and backed away down the trail, hoping that the other boy would not follow to disturb the special place below.

———————————————

Daddy was sitting on the back porch when Elam came up from the canyon.

"Where you been?" Daddy called. "Your momma's been worried."

Elam pushed through the gate and climbed the steps into the yard. "Worried? What for?"

His father arose. "You didn't say anything about where you were going."

"Everybody was asleep."

"Elam! You've got to quit going off by yourself. You just can't do it. Not around here." He shook his head. "Why do you insist on being alone all the time? Ever since Brett died you've just —"

Elam thrust his hands over his ears. "How many times you gonna tell me that?" he shouted. "I'm sick to death of hearin' it."

Even with his hands clenched over his ears, he could hear his father's voice.

"Son! You've got to get past what's happened to you."

The pressure in Elam's head squeezed tears out the corners of his eyes. "It didn't happen to me!" he cried.

He felt a choking sensation rising up in his chest as he pushed past his father and into the house.

Daddy followed, but Momma intercepted him in the kitchen.

"Hank, he's all right," Elam heard her say as he fled to his room.

Chapter Thirteen

Elam sat on the edge of his bed and rummaged through the odds and ends in the old tobacco tin he had taken from his drawer. He reached in and pulled out an empty .22 casing. He sniffed at it. The smell of gunpowder still lingered within. The casing was slightly flattened on one side where he and Brett had hammered at it with rocks, trying to pry the bullet from its shell. Elam wondered where the slug had ended up after they triggered its firing. He remembered the surprised expression on Brett's face after the explosion.

"You dead?" Brett had asked.

"No, you?" was Elam's reply.

He dropped the casing back into the tin and looked at the clock. Not yet noon.

Last night had been Daddy's first shift on grave-yard, so Elam had decided to keep to his room today, not wanting to disturb his father's daytime sleep. He figured if he stayed inside his father could rest without worry or complaint. But the day crept by, inching along with the sunlight crossing his room.

He pulled a folded map from the tin. The map had been sketched in pencil on coarse grade school paper. On it Brett had marked the region's best fishing spots according to the time of year.

Later, Elam had written in "May 12" by a certain bend of the pencil-drawn river.

Elam refolded the map and tucked it back into its place. Then he returned the tobacco tin to his top drawer, behind the folded tee shirts.

The clock on his bedside table seemed to be stuck on 11:48. Elam picked it up and shook it, listening to the rattle of gears and springs. He wound it tight, wishing that would hurry the time along. He shoved his hands into his pockets and paced the floor, measuring the width of the room with his stride.

Chapter Fourteen

One day of pent-up solitude was enough. Today Elam had to get outside, even if it meant another lecture from his father on the dangers of loneliness.

He stood on the back porch and watched the morning sunlight spread down the hillside into the canyon. The realization struck him that from the first day he had stepped into this ghost-ridden country he hadn't once been alone, except for yesterday, when he had kept to his room. Something beyond vision had always been there to dog his steps and accompany his uninvited intrusions into the arid landscape.

Today was no different. As he crept down into the canyon, he could feel the desert itself alive and breathing, thriving on the dry air that made his own breath shallow and short. Even the wash seemed to flow with sibilant murmurings. He was so absorbed in the brooding life around him that he was caught by surprise when two boys jumped out from the bushes.

"Hey! Where you goin'?"

Elam jerked to a halt. He recognized the speaker. It was the one the others had called Dicky. He was accompanied by the tall, sandy-haired boy that Elam had run away from days earlier. Together they blocked his way.

"You live in the house on the point, don't you?" the tall boy asked.

Elam frowned in confusion. "The point?"

"The last house on the road. The point."

"Oh. Yeah. That's where I live."

The tall boy nodded. "I thought so. Your dad works at the plant with my dad. I'm Mike Richards."

Elam shielded his eyes from the sun. "My—my name is Elam."

A snort escaped from Dicky. "Elam? What kind of name is that?"

Elam scowled in annoyance. "My grandpa was named—"

He was interrupted by a shout from the hillside behind him.

"Dicky! Mike! You find it yet?"

The voice was followed by noises in the brush— grunts and curses and cracking branches.

"Over here," Dicky called.

Elam took a deep breath. "My grandpa was named Elam," he said, letting the breath out. Then he cleared his throat. "What . . . what are you looking for?" Though he asked, he thought he could guess the answer.

"A coyote trap," Mike said. He glanced back over his shoulder. "We had it set back there in the wash."

"Yeah," added Dicky. "There's a fifty-dollar bounty on coyote skins. We're gonna catch one and—"

"It wasn't a coyote trap," Elam mumbled.

"—and get the—"

"Shut up, Dicky." Mike turned to Elam. "What did you say?"

Elam backed away. "It was a bear trap."

Mike took a step forward. "How do you know? Did you see it?"

Elam felt a pressure building up in his chest—a desire to turn and run, to flee from the questions that stirred up so many unpleasant memories. *How do you know? Did you see it?*

Elam rattled his head to clear out the old images. He thought instead of the coyote and what the trap would have done to it. "Yeah, I saw it. Right where you left it."

"We left it hidden. Covered up in sand."

"It was right there. Right where you left it! It— it had been sprung."

Dicky's face brightened. "We caught something?"

Elam spun about at the stumbling sounds behind him. Another boy emerged into the wash, red-faced and sweating.

The boy gasped for breath. "There you guys are."

Elam shook his head at Dicky's question. "No, you didn't catch anything! It was just sprung."

The new boy passed Elam, jerking his thumb at him.

"Who's this?" he asked.

"His name's Elam," answered Mike. "He says he knows where the trap is."

The boy looked Elam over. "Oh, yeah?"

"That's not what I said. I don't know where it is. I didn't take it."

Mike ignored the correction. "He says somebody sprung it. I bet it was Refúgio."

"Stupid Mexican," said Dicky. "He's always messin' things up."

"Refúgio?" Elam thought of the dark-skinned boy he had seen the other day.

"Yeah," said Mike. "Refúgio. I'll bet he's still around. Come on! Let's see if we can find him."

Without another word, the three boys took off down the wash at a run. Elam held his breath, watching as they raced toward the gully that led to the hidden pine sapling. But they ignored the turn up the hillside and kept heading straight along the wash.

"Refúgio," Elam said, breathing the name out with his sigh of relief.

———— —— ————

"I found a friend today," Elam said at the dinner table.

His father stopped in mid-bite and set his fork down on his plate.

"A friend? Really?" His forehead wrinkled up with a hopeful look.

Elam nodded.

"That's good," his father continued. "That's real good."

"His name is Refúgio."

"Refúgio? What kind of name is that?"

"He's a Mexican."

"What? A Mexican? I didn't mean for you to . . ." Daddy's voice trailed off, and he shook his head. After a moment he continued. "You've gotta be smarter than that about choosing your friends."

Elam felt confused. "But . . . I thought—" He could feel the pressure rising in his chest again. He looked to his mother for help.

She gave him a reassuring nod and turned to face Daddy. "Hank," she said. "At least he's met someone he likes. Isn't that what we wanted?"

Daddy picked up his fork to continue eating. "He just needs to be careful who he makes friends with, that's all I'm saying."

Elam shoved back from the table, gathered up his plate and cup, and carried them to the sink. He rinsed them and set them on the counter. Then he pushed through the front door, wondering what it would take to make his father happy.

As he sat on the porch, he heard the door open behind him. It closed with a rattle.

"Son?"

His mother sat down on the step beside him.

"Tell me about your new friend," she said.

Elam didn't know what to say. He had never even talked to the boy. He stared at the orange sky that silhouetted the houses on the far ridge. "I think he's a lot like Brett," he finally offered, though he couldn't explain why.

Chapter Fifteen

From where Elam stood at the top of the hill the bubbling spring was hidden—concealed by a rim of rock and thorny growth. He caught his breath after the hurried climb and let his gaze dart across the lower slope. He couldn't escape the nagging feeling that he had just missed Refúgio.

So it had been all morning. Elam had hunted through the canyon, convinced that Refúgio was somewhere near, resting in the shade of a palo verde, drinking from the growing pool that surrounded the pine tree, racing across the rough and tumbled hillsides.

As Elam rounded each rocky outcropping or threaded his way through another thorny knot of mesquite and tumbleweed, anticipation built up within him, only to be dashed away by the feeling of a near miss — as if the spot were still warm from the Mexican boy's presence.

With that feeling strong in his mind, Elam crested the hill and ranged across the opposite slope, searching for any sign that a pair of worn cowboy boots had passed this way.

At first the tangled movement beneath the creosote bush confused him. It appeared as if some ancient, scale-armored creature were struggling against the coils of a rattlesnake. As Elam stared in fascination, he realized that he was watching the rattler shed its own old and tattered husk.

He crept nearer for a better view. The cast-off skin looked as delicate as ashes from a burned-up mountain fern. In great ripples, the snake shrugged out of its dead scales, at last wriggling free. Its new skin glistened. The colors stood out in shiny blacks, browns, and grays against the dusty ground.

Elam inched closer.

The snake raised up and flicked its tongue at him. Then it bobbed its head, untangled its coiled body, and glided back into the shadows, flowing water-like over the rocks and sand.

Elam watched until it disappeared. When he turned to retrace his steps up the hill, his heart jumped. Another boy stood just up the rise, staring down at him with dark eyes.

"May I take the snakeskin?" he asked with a light Spanish accent.

Though Elam recognized the boy, surprise pulled the question out of him before he had a chance to collect himself. "Who—who are you?"

"My name is Refúgio." The boy wiped his hands on his canvas pants. "And you?" He thrust his right hand forward.

Elam muttered his own name, staring at the offered hand.

"Elam," repeated Refúgio. "Pleased to meet you." He reached for Elam's hand and shook it vigorously. His eyes sparkled beneath the dark hair that hung down on his forehead.

Elam pulled his hand back. "Uh, me too," he said.

Refúgio squatted on his heels and peered beneath the creosote bush. "It's a big one," he said. "The snake. Look at the skin."

Elam peeked over the boy's shoulder. "Yeah. It is."

"Do you want it?" Refúgio asked, abruptly standing up.

At home in the mountains Elam would have considered the snakeskin a prize. But here, with the desert looking on, taking the empty skin seemed too bold, almost disrespectful. "No. No thanks."

"You don't like snakes?"

"I like them fine, but—"

"May I take it then? The skin?"

"Sure, I guess." Elam wrinkled up his forehead. "What are you going to do with it?"

Refúgio bent down and cradled the empty husk in his hands, carefully lifting it from beneath the bush. "Maybe I'll make something from it."

"What could you make out of that?" The worn scales seemed too delicate and brittle for use.

Refúgio grinned. "A surprise."

Chapter sixteen

Elam dreamed again of rushing water. When daylight nudged him awake, the sound of it was still in
his ears, lingering just on the edge of hearing. He lay
on his pillow, face to the ceiling, and enjoyed the
rolling sensation that the chattering noise pushed
through him—the feeling of a river tumbling over
rocks. And he thought of Brett, rolling and tumbling
in the stream. He wondered again what Brett had
thought about, just before the darkness took him,
and if it had felt like falling out of the water. But
they had said that Brett was most likely unconscious
before he drowned, so it probably felt like nothing.

And then Elam was full awake. In a panic he
pushed those thoughts away, sitting up and stamp-
ing his bare feet on the floor to restore the day.

He forced a yawn and stretched, and the morning returned to normal.

He glanced out his bedroom window at the growing light and jumped up in surprise. A face peered back in at him. In relief he recognized Refúgio. Elam pulled on a pair of jeans and signaled for the other boy to meet him at the back door.

It was still early, just half-past six, so Daddy was not home from his shift at the smelter yet. But the time was short.

"Where you been?" Elam asked as he opened the screen door. It had been nearly a week since Elam had watched him retreat across a dusty hillside, cradling the newly shed snakeskin in his hands.

Refúgio held up the bundle he had been carrying under his arm. "I made you something." The package was wrapped in a soiled gunnysack.

"How'd you know where I lived?"

"You're new here. And this house was the empty one."

Elam nodded at the logic. "Hurry, come on in while I finish getting dressed. My dad will be home soon."

He led the way through the kitchen.

Momma was there at the stove, fixing breakfast.

"Momma," Elam said. "This is my friend, Refúgio. I told you about him."

She glanced at the wall clock and then looked

back at the Mexican boy. "Nice to meet you," she said. "Would you like to have some oatmeal with Elam?"

"I've already eaten," he answered. "But thank you anyway."

The two boys hurried to the bedroom. Elam pulled a tee shirt over his head and fished a pair of mismatched socks out of his drawer. "Okay, so what's that you've got in the bag?"

Refúgio unwrapped the burlap package and lay its contents on the bed.

"From the snakeskin," he said. "And an empty cigar box."

The snakeskin covered the box, adorning it with diamond patterns of desert color—browns, blacks, and grays.

"For you," Refúgio said.

Elam picked up the box and ran his finger over its covering. He had thought the castoff skin would be dry and brittle, but instead it felt smooth to the touch, hard and tough.

"How did you do this?" he asked.

"It's a secret." Refúgio smiled, his face wrinkling up with the strength of it, making him look almost ancient. It was a contagious smile, and Elam had to look away to keep from grinning himself.

"Why for me?" he asked.

"Because you were there."

Something in the way Refúgio spoke — the melodious accent, the quiet tones, the shining eyes — brought back this morning's waking memories.

"No I wasn't," Elam whispered. "Not 'til it was too late."

And then he shook his head. "You mean I was there for the snake — to see it shed?"

Refúgio shrugged. "Of course. What else?"

"That was somethin'. Like he was being born brand new."

Elam raised the lid of the box. Inside, he found a scrap of paper folded in amongst the tobacco smells. In blue ink and a spidery hand were scrawled the words: *Made by Refúgio Gúzman de Ortiz. July 1961.*

"Thanks," he said.

"*De nada.*"

"What?"

"*De nada.* You're welcome."

Elam nodded. "*De nada.* How do you say thank you?"

"*Gracias.*"

"*Gracias,* then." He closed the box and examined its covering once again, inspecting the tucked corners and the neatly folded seams. "My dad will be home soon. He'll . . . he's working graveyard, and he'll want to sleep. I'll hurry and eat, then we can go before he gets home."

He set the snakeskin box on his dresser and led Refúgio out of the room.

Momma had a bowl of steaming cereal ready on the table for him, as if she, too, wanted to hurry them out of the house.

The distant whistle from the smelter announced the shift change.

Elam sat on the edge of his chair and shoveled the oatmeal into his mouth. He scooped up the last spoonful, wiped his mouth with his hand, and gulped down his milk.

"Let's go," he said.

By ten after seven the screen door had slammed shut behind them, and they were off into the canyon, Elam leading the way.

Refúgio stopped at the mouth of the hidden alcove. "*¡Hijo de la —*"

Even Elam had trouble recognizing the place. The pond now spread from wall to wall and had begun to overflow its basin, the stream creeping down the gully a good distance before being swallowed by the sand. The pine tree stood on its island, rising five feet above the ferns and skunk cabbage that had begun to grow around it.

"How . . . where did this come from?" Refúgio asked.

Elam grinned. "I found it. It's just like home."

Refúgio kicked off one boot and then the other. "It's like magic," he said, stepping out into the water in his bare feet. He laughed out loud. "And it's cold!" He turned to face Elam. "How could this be?" And then he fell over backwards into the pool, his face vanishing beneath the surface.

"Be careful!" Elam cried, springing forward.

Refúgio sat up and blew water from his mouth and nose, shaking the wet tangles of his hair.

"Did you make this?" he asked, a look of wonder on his face.

Elam swallowed down the sudden panic he had felt at Refúgio's disappearance. Then he shook his head impatiently. "No, of course not. How could I?"

"You could have brought the tree. You came from the mountains. You could have brought it with you. A magic tree that makes water right from the ground. That—"

"No! It's not magic. It was just here. My father wouldn't have let me bring something like this from home, magic or not." Elam batted his hand out as if that absurd idea were hanging in the air between them. "He wouldn't allow it. This was what he was taking me away from. To be replaced by that." Elam swept his arm out, indicating the desert.

Refúgio sloshed out of the pool, wringing the water from his tee shirt. "You make your father sound cruel."

Elam bit his lip. "No. It's not that. He . . . he just doesn't understand." Elam slumped back against the basin wall. "Maybe he thought he was helping. But I don't need the help. Momma said I was going to be fine, but Daddy said I needed a change, that I needed friends, that I needed . . . "

He looked at Refúgio, looked into his dark brown eyes. Those eyes seemed deep enough to hold any secret he wanted to tell.

He sighed. "I just need to go home."

Refúgio wiped a dribble of water off his nose. "Home?" he said, turning to look into the basin.

Elam followed his gaze back to the green pine, tucked away in its sheltered spot, growing up through the other impossible plants.

Refúgio pointed at it with his chin. "You bring it with you, it seems."

Elam shook his head. "I told you, it was just here."

Refúgio's forehead wrinkled up with a doubtful look. "Somebody had to put it there. It couldn't just grow from nothing. Maybe those gringo boys, Dicky and Mike?"

Elam stood up and looked out across the canyon. "I don't even think they know it's here."

"Good, then," Refúgio said. "To them it would just be another thing to spoil."

That night, Elam carefully transferred his collected memories from the tobacco tin to the new snakeskin box. He examined each item in its turn, holding on to the photograph of Brett the longest. At last he lay the picture in the box faceup and, as an afterthought, placed the empty tin beside it. He closed the lid, and his thoughts turned from Brett to Refúgio, the one image merging into the other, like the shadowy reflections of a pond changing into bright sparkles of sunlight.

He placed the box in the drawer where the tin had been, buried back behind his folded clothes.

The night was late, and the coyotes had already begun their yammering. Elam climbed into bed and listened to their mournful wails, each one echoing back the cries of the others.

"Goodnight," he whispered to them, glad that their noise was there to keep him company.

Chapter Seventeen

"What do the coyotes find to eat around here?" Elam asked. He and Refúgio sat in the shade of the cottonwood at the edge of Elam's back yard. The morning had faded into noon, and the blazing sun stood high overhead.

Refúgio pulled at a bull-headed thorn, yanking it out of the ground, root and all. "Everything," he said. "Mostly rabbits, I guess. But my grandfather says they'll eat whatever they can catch. Birds. Snakes. Lizards. But not horny toads."

"How come not horny toads?"

"They squirt blood out of their eyes."

"Naw!" Elam dismissed the ridiculous notion with a shake of his head. "They don't. How could they do that?"

"They do." Refúgio pulled up another thorn plant. "And the coyotes don't like it. It makes them sick."

"How do you know?"

"My grandfather told me."

Elam still felt skeptical. "Does he know everything?"

"He's old. He knows a lot. He knows that the coyotes howl because they don't like the night to be empty. He knows how to find water in the desert and how to catch rattlesnakes with his bare hands." Refúgio sat up straighter. His eyes sparkled as he talked of his grandfather. "He knows how to live where there is no living."

Elam leaned back on his elbows to get a better view of Refúgio's profile. "My grandpa was a cowboy," he offered. "I was named after him."

Refúgio laughed. "Mine is part Indian."

"Oh. Does he mind if you're friends with me?"

"No. Why should he?"

Elam shrugged. "Where's your house?" he asked. "You never told me where you live."

Refúgio looked up through the leaves of the cottonwood. "I prefer being outside." He jumped to his feet. "Let's go see your tree, how much it's grown."

Chapter Eighteen

For the first time since Elam had been in the desert, clouds obscured the afternoon sun. Gray and purple billows mounted up against the sky. The dusty tang of rain hung in the air, acrid in his nostrils.

To his surprise, even with the sun hidden, the heat remained intense — magnified if that were possible — by the roiling cloud cover. The hair on his arms stood on end as if the air were charged with electricity.

He stood at the back door and shivered.

"Good day to stay in," Momma said, putting a hand on his shoulder. "You'd be wise to stay out of that canyon."

"But I've got to meet Refúgio. We have something to do today."

"It can wait."

"I'll bring him here if it starts to rain."

Momma wiped her cheek with the back of her hand. "It's not the rain that worries me."

"Oh, Daddy'll be asleep for another couple of hours at least."

Momma shook her head. "Nor that neither. It's the flood that can come scooting through that canyon without any warning. It doesn't even have to be raining here for it to come."

Elam stepped out the door into the heavy air. "Then let me hurry down and get him."

Before his mother had a chance to protest he dashed across the yard, leapt down the stairs, and pushed through the back gate.

"I'll be quick," he called back.

With the gloomy overcast, Elam felt like he was descending into an alien landscape. An eerie thrill surged through him as he threaded his way down the hillside. Each cactus, each scrubby bush and tree bristled in the greenish half-light. A distant roll of thunder rumbled across the sky. A nearer one answered.

As Elam stepped down into the wash, his mother's warning came back to him. An electric tingle brushed along his spine. In relief he spied Refúgio trudging toward him in the sand.

"Refúgio! Over here! Let's get up to my house before it starts to rain."

Refúgio stopped and glanced at Elam. A strange look spread across his face. He called out something that Elam couldn't understand, the words garbled by the rising wind.

Elam hurried toward him. "What did you say?"

The first huge drops of water exploded on the ground between them.

Refúgio cupped his hands around his mouth. "I said they've found it. Dicky and Michael." He dashed the rain out of his eyes. "They found it!"

A crack of thunder split the sky above them. Elam involuntarily ducked, and he stumbled into Refúgio's arms.

"They found the pine tree?" he asked, regaining his balance. "They found the pool?"

Refúgio shook his head. "No." The wind pushed at them now, shoving them back in the direction from which Refúgio had come. Rain flashed out of the sky, pelting down, obscuring their surroundings.

"They found the trap," Refúgio said.

He shifted aside. Through the watery haze, Elam could just make out a tan mound lying still in the middle of the wash.

"They . . . they found the trap?"

Refúgio nodded. "I thought I hid it well. They must have—"

Elam sprinted toward the place, but there was nothing he could do. The bear trap had snapped shut around the coyote's head, crushing its skull. Rain beat down on the animal now, matting its fur and washing away the blood and gore.

A piece of bologna protruded from the coyote's mouth. Elam tore the meat free and flung it away into the bushes, feeling nausea wash through him.

"They killed it!" he shouted. "Those . . . they killed it!"

He dropped to his knees and let the downpour pound against him. Gusts of wind whipped along the canyon, driving the rain into his face, smearing the tears back away from his eyes. A flash of white light and an immediate crack of thunder drove him to the ground.

Refúgio pulled him up. "We better get out of here," he shouted. "It's getting bad."

"But what'll we do with the coyote? We can't let them have it."

"We'll come back for it later."

Refúgio pushed at Elam, driving him out of the wash and up the slope. Lightning blazed across the sky, accompanied by ear-splitting thunder. Elam felt that he was climbing through a solid wall of water, each breath becoming a struggle to separate the air from the pelting rain. Rivulets cascaded down the hillside around them, making the hill slippery. He looked back, but the wash was invisible in the downpour.

By the time they staggered into his yard, the fury of the storm had lessened a bit. Daddy was waiting at the back door, his face dark with anger. He stepped aside and held the door open as they hurried in. Momma draped a towel over each of them.

"At least try to drip on the rug," Daddy said. "And take off those shoes."

Elam could hear the impatience in his voice. He was sure Daddy was only holding his temper in check because of Refúgio, unwilling to express himself in front of a stranger.

"You've worried your mother," he said. "Didn't she tell you to stay in?"

Elam wiped his face with the towel. "I had to get Refúgio. He was waiting for me."

Daddy grunted.

Refúgio nodded at the door. "This storm is early. The cloudbursts don't usually begin until August."

"Elam," Momma said. "You boys should get some dry clothes on. Refúgio can wear something of yours."

Daddy cleared his throat, about to speak, but Elam pulled Refúgio along into his room.

Behind the closed door they peeled out of their wet clothes. Elam provided dry underwear, a pair of jeans, and an extra tee shirt.

"You can bring them back tomorrow," he said.

Refúgio laughed. "If I can get home without losing them." He hiked the pants up with one hand. "Do you have some rope?"

Elam laughed, too. "You're even skinnier than me. How about a belt?"

By the time they were dressed, the rain no longer hammered on the tin roof of the house, and only distant rumbles of thunder interrupted the quiet after the storm.

Elam was hesitant to leave his room, unsure what Daddy might do. He would likely wait until Refúgio left to say anything about "proper friends," but Elam didn't want to take any chances.

"I've found a good use for your box," he said. "The one you made."

He pulled it out of the drawer and handed it to Refúgio. "I've put my things in it."

Refúgio opened the box. He held up the photograph of Brett. "Who's this?" he asked.

Elam took the picture from him as if to examine it more closely. "Oh, just a friend."

Refúgio nodded. "From up in the mountains?"

"Uh-huh."

"You ever going to go back up there for a visit?"

"Someday."

"He will be glad to see you."

Elam handed the picture back. "Probably."

Refúgio replaced the photo in the box and closed the lid. "My grandfather taught me how to do this, how to make the box. He says the snakeskin is lucky, because snakes live forever." He grinned. "That's what he says, but I've seen a rattler run over on the highway before."

Elam looked out the window at the tattered clouds. The desert sky beyond the clouds was bluer than he had ever seen it. As blue as the sky beyond Mount Baldy. So blue it no longer seemed flat and close and lifeless. Instead it was as deep as he imagined heaven might be.

"My friend won't be there when I go back," he said. "He's dead."

———

Refúgio was quiet as he and Elam made their way to where they had left the trap. Since the mention of Brett's death, Refúgio had barely spoken, except to suggest that the weather had cleared enough to see to the coyote.

Elam had become accustomed to silence, so Refúgio's manner suited him. With a shovel carried against his shoulder, he trudged along next to the Mexican boy.

The rain had taken the edge off the heat of the afternoon, but now the sun reappeared, sucking the moisture into the sky, turning the air heavy and humid. The smell of damp earth and new-watered greenery was a pleasant change, but still Elam squirmed in discomfort at the stickiness under his shirt.

As they neared the place, it seemed to Elam that the coyote must have nearly washed away in the downpour. From a distance it appeared as a gray-brown mound plastered against the sand.

"I hate those guys," he said through gritted teeth. "Look what they've done."

Refúgio nodded in assent. He dropped to his knees beside the animal. "We've got to remove the trap," he said.

But that became a grisly task. The trap's spring was strong, and with the coyote in the way, it was difficult to get leverage with only their hands and fingers.

"Maybe we should just bury them together," Elam suggested, glancing up at the buzzards now spiraling overhead.

"No," answered Refúgio. "We can't do that to him."

Elam nodded. He ducked his head to rub his cheek against his shoulder, then he went back to work.

Finally, using the shovel as a wedge, he managed to pry the metal jaws just wide enough for Refúgio to wrestle the coyote out and away from the trap.

Elam sat back in the damp sand and wiped the sweat from his forehead. "Now what? Where we gonna bury him?"

"I know a place." Refúgio rolled the carcass onto the burlap bag they had brought from Elam's house. Then he lifted the bundle in his arms. Without another word, he headed along the wash to a point where the valley widened a bit, forming a broader floor. He left the sand and threaded his way through a stand of ragged bushes. The dirt here was softer than on the hillsides — topsoil that had washed down and accumulated over centuries of thundershowers and pounding rain.

Refúgio led the way across the flat space, almost to the rising slope. He lay his burden on the ground.

"Here," he said, taking the shovel from Elam. He easily pushed the shovel into the wet earth with his booted foot.

The two took turns digging until the hole was more than three feet deep.

"That should be enough," Elam said.

They lowered the coyote into the hole and gently pushed the soil in, covering the animal, hiding it from the desert scavengers.

As Elam tamped down the last shovelful of dirt, Refúgio cleared his throat as if to speak. But then he looked away, up at the sky, seemingly intent on the buzzards circling off in the distance. At last he stammered out his question: "Your friend . . . your friend is dead?"

Elam was confused for a moment, thinking he meant the coyote. But then he remembered. Brett. He nodded, expecting the familiar questions: how, when, where.

But Refúgio was silent again, as if he were unsure how to continue. After a moment he asked, "Does it still hurt?"

Elam felt a thickening in his chest, not just at the sudden memories that Refúgio's words recalled, but at the softness of his voice and the nature of his question. It was one he hadn't heard at all through that last long year. He nodded again.

Refúgio tugged at the neck of his tee shirt. "Do you—" he paused as if weighing his words "—do you think your tree has survived the rain?"

Surprised at the sudden change in subject, Elam glanced over his shoulder in the direction of the hidden basin. "Maybe we should check on it," he said.

———————————————

As they climbed the gully toward the basin, Elam began to worry about what they might find. The cloudburst had washed the sand of the gully smooth and eaten at the banks so that chunks of muddy earth had sloughed off in its wake. Before long they were sloshing ankle deep through standing water. Elam hurried on, but as he climbed into the alcove he discovered his concern was unfounded.

The mouth of the basin had washed away with the runoff from the storm. The pool was gone but the tree still stood, now taller than Elam, the center of a sandy bowl.

Elam's mouth dropped open in surprise. Irises had shot up, crowding the edges of the bowl, their green, spear-like leaves reaching toward the sun. And they were in full bloom, their blues and purples reflecting the depth of the sky overhead.

"It's . . . it's not possible," he said. "It's not."

"It's magic," whispered Refúgio.

———————————————

On the way back to Elam's house, Refúgio stopped to retrieve the trap.

"This time they won't find it again," he said.

He dropped the trap into the burlap bag and slung it over his shoulder. Its muffled clanking accompanied them as they trudged up the hillside.

Elam walked alongside deep in thought. Daddy had friends back home who made their living trapping animals, grown men who hunted the streams and ponds, setting their lines, claiming their bounty. Elam had thought nothing of it. But what he saw today was different.

"They didn't need to kill that coyote," he said. Then he shuddered. The image of the dead animal, lying plastered to the ground, seemed to be burned into his mind. "Why would they do that?"

Refúgio paused and looked back down into the canyon. "Just to see if they could, I guess."

Elam followed Refúgio's gaze. "That's a stupid reason."

Refúgio shrugged and started climbing again.

Elam followed, his thoughts now taking a different track. After a moment he said, "Me and Brett tried to open a bullet once by pounding it with rocks—just to see if we could."

Refúgio's shoulders shook as if with a brief laugh. "That was stupid," he said.

"Yeah. I guess it was."

"Could you?"

It was Elam's turn to laugh. "Yeah. Sort of."

It was nearing suppertime when Elam opened the gate into the back yard.

"You wanna stay to dinner?" he asked. "I'll see if it's okay." He hurried across the yard without waiting for Refúgio's reply.

"Mom," he called through the screen door. "Can Refúgio eat with us?"

Elam heard a chair scrape on the kitchen floor. Daddy appeared at the door. "I'd rather not," he said.

"Why?" Elam asked.

Daddy opened the screen door for Elam. "I've told you why. He's got his own friends, you should have yours."

"But . . ." Elam looked back over his shoulder, feeling his face flush with embarrassment.

Refúgio nodded. He turned away and headed down the walk and out the gate.

Chapter Nineteen

Elam lay on his back on the covers of his bed and stared at the ceiling, thinking of pine trees and irises growing where they had no right to be. It was as if the ghosts of the desert were trying to entice him with bits and pieces of a home that was beyond his reach. He feared that if he shared the wonder of it with his parents it would all vanish, just like Refúgio had disappeared after Daddy's rudeness the other night.

Refúgio had simply walked away. The next day the clothes Elam loaned him had appeared on the front porch neatly folded. That was three days ago, and Elam had not seen Refúgio since.

Nor had he spoken to his father. Daddy was back to working days at the smelter. He left home at six-thirty in the morning and returned by three-thirty in the afternoon. Elam avoided the house then, not coming in until dinnertime. He kept his anger with Daddy to himself, letting it shrink into a small knot in the back of his mind.

He grunted at the memory of it, then slipped off the bed, opened his drawer, and pulled out the snakeskin box. He lifted out the photograph of Brett. Conversation with his best friend had always come easy, almost as if they shared the same mind. Perhaps that had come from living nearly their whole lives together.

"What should I do?" he whispered to the photograph.

There was no answer.

Elam put the picture away. He glanced out his bedroom window. "Maybe I should go find Refúgio."

But Elam had no idea where to look. Refúgio had never told him where he lived. He always changed the subject, preferring to talk about other things. So Elam had been waiting for him to come back on his own. Today, he would take matters into his own hands.

As he stepped out the back gate, he spied Dicky, Mike, and another of the neighbor boys sauntering toward him down the road. It was too late to duck back behind the wall.

"Hey!" Mike called with a wave. "Where you been?" He carried a metal cylinder, slung back against his shoulder like a rifle.

Elam let the gate swing shut behind him. "Around."

Dicky strutted forward. "You ever see a carbide cannon before?"

"A what?" Elam asked.

"A carbide cannon. We're going out to the point to shoot it."

Mike patted the thing on his shoulder. "This. It's a carbide cannon. My big brother made it."

The third boy shook the paper sack he carried, producing a tinny rattle. "We've got plenty of ammo. Come on."

Elam's curiosity got the best of him, and so despite his dislike of these boys, he followed, past his house to where the road ended at the curved point of the ridge.

Mike laid the metal tube against a rock, aimed out over the desert slope. It was an old, cast-iron fence post that had been plugged at one end with cement. Dicky pulled a water-filled Coke bottle from his back pocket. The other boy emptied his paper sack, spilling red-and-white–labeled soup cans across the ground.

Mike produced another can with a screwed-on

lid. "Carbide," he said, holding up the can. "Just add water and —"

"Kaboom!" shouted Dicky.

Elam shook his head. He knew what carbide was. "Isn't that kind of dangerous?"

"Naw," answered Dicky. "We do it all the time."

Mike shook a few small, gray granules from the can into the tube. "My brother once blew a tennis ball clear across the canyon."

Dicky snorted. "That's nothing. My brother shot a jackrabbit out of one."

Mike slugged him in the arm. "Liar."

"Ow. Did, too. All they found were the ears. Kaboom!"

In Elam's mind Dicky's explosive imitation turned to thunder. Lightning flashed, illuminating the bedraggled form of the dead coyote. "Is that all you think about?" he growled. "Killing things?"

Dicky's exuberance faded. "Huh?"

Elam clenched his fists. "You killed that coyote."

"What are you talking about?" Dicky always seemed to have that same pinched expression on his face. Suddenly Elam hated it.

"With that trap! You killed the coyote!"

"Whoa." Mike straightened up from his fiddling with the cannon. "What do you mean? Did we *really* catch something?"

Dicky jumped and spun about in excitement. "We caught a coyote? Yahoo! Fifty bucks!"

Mike grabbed Dicky's shirt and shook him still. He turned to Elam. "What do you know about it? Where is it?"

Elam felt the muscles in his jaw clench. "We buried it!"

"What?" Dicky sputtered, straining against Mike's grasp. "You buried it? But it was ours!"

Mike released Dicky's shirt and stepped toward Elam.

Elam stood his ground, staring into Mike's face.

"We actually caught something?" Mike asked, his forehead wrinkling up with the question. "You saw it?"

"You smashed its skull in." Elam glared at the taller boy. "That was a bear trap you used."

"And you buried it?" Dicky repeated. "How could—"

"Shut up," Mike said, casting a warning glance over his shoulder. He faced Elam again. "A real coyote?"

Elam nodded uncertainly. He had expected anger from the other boy. Instead he saw confused disbelief on Mike's face.

"Yeah, a coyote." Elam stepped back, trying to salvage his own rage. "And we buried it!"

"We?" asked Mike. "We, who?"

"Me and Refúgio."

Mike nodded slowly. "I guess bologna works after all."

"But what about our fifty bucks?" Dicky said.

"Who was gonna skin it?" Mike asked.

"I woulda," Dicky replied.

Mike grunted.

"I would," Dicky insisted.

Mike ignored him and turned his attention back to Elam. "You're friends with Refúgio?"

Elam still felt defiance boiling within him. "Yeah."

Dicky snorted. "You gonna go play with him today?"

"I would if I knew where he lived!" Elam's anger made tears squeeze out the corner of his eyes. He spun about and headed back toward his own house.

"I think he lives over in San Pedro," Mike called after him.

"Yeah," Dicky said. "That's where *all* the Mexicans live." And then he snickered. "Or out with the coyotes. The way he smells, he's probably one of those ranch kids."

Dicky yelped as Mike slugged him again.

Later that day, Elam stood alone at the trestle bridge and looked across to the far side. The road climbed up the opposite hill and disappeared beyond the rise. He studied the bridge. It was built of massive timbers and surfaced with thick wooden planks. Railings stretched along each side of the single-car track, and a narrow walkway ran along the left side, protected from a fall into the canyon by another, shoulder-high railing. The bridge smelled of creosote and motor oil.

Elam stepped onto the walkway.

He had crossed over with Momma several times before, riding with her into town, to the grocery store or the post office. But he had not been interested in crossing on his own. Until today.

He hurried along, relieved at the solidity he felt beneath his feet, as if the bridge were part of the earth itself. He climbed up the opposite road, followed it along another ridge, passed by the small company-run hospital, and descended into town. He headed straight for the grocery store, pushed through its door into the cool, dim interior, and approached the Mexican woman who sat behind the counter.

He pulled a scrap of paper from his pocket. Glancing at it, he said, "I'm looking for Refúgio Gúzman de Ortiz. Do you know where he lives?"

The woman smiled. "Refúgio? Let me think. I know several Gúzman families." She stared at the ceiling for a moment, then shook her head. "No. I don't know any Refúgio Gúzman."

Elam shifted from one foot to the other. "Can you tell me where San Pedro is then?"

The woman laughed. "Why, just follow the street." She turned and pointed through the large window. "Up that way."

Elam could make out the backs of small houses clustered haphazardly along a tree-covered hill. "Thank you," he said. And then he corrected himself. *"Gracias."*

"De nada," the woman answered, bowing slightly.

Elam discovered that San Pedro was actually a street name. It was the main thoroughfare that led through the Mexican side of town. Wooden houses crowded the street. Dirt roads wandered off the main avenue to more dilapidated dwellings. Despite the rundown nature of many of the homes, the thing that struck Elam about this place was the color. Not only were trees and flowering bushes more abundant than in other parts of town, but the houses themselves were brightly painted in vibrant blues and greens. It was as if the people who lived here had found a way to get the better of the dry, dusty desert.

Elam walked along the road. A group of kids playing in the street stopped their game to watch him pass. Elam spotted a pair of old men sitting hunched over a small table in front of what appeared to be a restaurant.

He hesitated just a moment, then hurried toward them. They were playing dominoes in the shade of a window awning.

"Excuse me," he said.

They glanced up.

"I'm looking for Refúgio Gúzman de Ortiz. Do you know him? He's my age. About twelve."

The man on Elam's left shook his head and muttered something in Spanish through a bristling white mustache. The other answered in a thick accent. "Gúzman? No. No. No Refúgio. I know Pablito y Luís, *pero no* Refúgio."

Elam thanked them and turned back to the street. A small girl with long black braids and dark eyes stood there, scratching her nose. "My brother is Refúgio," she said.

"He is?"

"Yes. Refúgio Ramírez."

Elam returned home just before dinner. It appeared that Dicky had been right. Refúgio Gúzman de Ortiz must live outside the city limits on one of the sparse ranches Elam had seen scattered along the highway on their first drive into town.

As he lay in bed that night, drifting toward sleep, he realized that unless Refúgio came looking for him, he might never see the boy again. The angry knot in the back of his mind tightened.

Chapter Twenty

Several more days passed with no sign of Refúgio. Early on the first Thursday of August there was a knock on the back door. Elam raced from his room to answer it. Mike Richards stood there beyond the screen.

"We're going swimming," Mike said. "You wanna come?"

Elam hesitated, surprised at the offer. He looked past Mike, hoping somehow to see Refúgio standing at the gate. "Uh, no. I can't go. I've got a lot to do."

"Oh." Mike shrugged. "All right. Just thought I'd ask."

"Thanks."

Mike stepped off the porch, but then he paused and turned back. "Sorry about the coyote," he said. "Thanks for burying it." Then he continued on his way, leaving the sidewalk to cross the dry lawn and jump the fence into the Gardners' back yard.

Elam watched him leave. The apology surprised him, but he still wished it was Refúgio who had knocked.

After Mike disappeared, Elam got busy with the work he had set for himself that day. He crept across the back road, holding the empty bucket tightly so it wouldn't rattle, in case Mike or the other boys were somewhere near. He filled the bucket from the stream at the pine basin and hauled it along the canyon to water the irises he had transplanted at the head of the coyote's grave. With care, he poured the water around the green spears. Though recently planted, the irises were already thriving. Elam stepped back to admire their blue-and-purple blooms. They reminded him of the houses in San Pedro. Perhaps he should fetch more of the plants and place them at the foot of the grave as well.

He looked up at the sky. Maybe today the thunderheads that mounted in the far west would do more than bluster up against the horizon. Maybe they would again clear the heat-drawn haze out of the sky, allowing it to reflect the deep and vibrant colors of the irises.

With the bucket banging against his leg, Elam trudged back to the basin. Since the previous thunderstorm had washed away the pool, the stream trickled unhindered down the gully, reaching almost to the wash before it melted into the earth.

Not wanting to go all the way back home for the shovel, he worked with his hands, digging up several more irises from the moist ground. He set them in the bucket and leaned back to rest. In this place he could almost forget the desert that encircled him. The basin floor was now carpeted in a variety of familiar plants: skunk cabbage, sumac, bearberry, feathered ferns, and new-sprouted thistle. Their smells, mingling with that of the pine and moist earth, took him beyond his arid surroundings.

He closed his eyes.

You wanna go or not? he heard Brett say.

He mumbled something about being too comfortable to move. "Go yourself," he added. "But bring me back a rainbow."

A startling crack shook him out of his reverie. A blinding flash and another boom of thunder brought him to his feet. The rain burst out of the sky, drenching him before he had a chance to move. He looked about, frantic.

Already the stream flowing from above had turned muddy, its oozing trickle transforming into a storm-fed torrent. The flood rose around his feet. He leapt out of the alcove and raced down the gully, splashing through the mounting current.

He came to a skidding halt at the wash. His way was blocked by what was now a raging river, thick with gray-brown mud and desert flotsam. And still the rain poured from the sky.

Elam feared that the rising stream tumbling down the gully would sweep him into the stronger course, so he scrambled up the bank, clutching at the overhanging palo verde. But the wet made its smooth bark slippery, and the mud of the bank gave him no purchase. He slid back down and felt the ground giving way beneath his feet. He clawed at the air in his panic, and then he choked as the water sucked him down.

His mind tumbled from darkness to glimmering light. He rolled over, and the bright images flared again—a figure standing against the sun, wavering in the watery light, as if seen from beneath a sparkling pool: Brett, standing, waiting.

Elam rolled once more, buffeted by the current, and the figure flickered into his sight again, this time reaching out with dark-skinned hands.

And then Elam felt a sudden jerk pulling him up out of the torrent. He gasped for air, coughing and sputtering. Another pull, and he found himself sprawled on solid ground. He retched, water streaming from his mouth and nose.

"Are you all right?" he heard a voice say.

But the violent fit of trembling that shook him prevented his answer. He looked about, trying to orient himself, to stop the spinning and tumbling in his mind.

His eyes settled on Refúgio squatting at his side, and that image gave him something to cling to. He clutched at Refúgio's arm, steadying himself while the rain continued to pound down upon them.

"Don't go away," Elam whispered hoarsely. "Don't go away again."

Refúgio pulled him to his feet. "Higher ground," he said. "Come on."

The air split with another flash and a crack of thunder. Together Refúgio and Elam staggered up the slope and crawled into the sparse protection of a leaning mesquite to wait out the storm.

And then the downpour stopped as suddenly as it had begun. The wall of rain moved up the slope behind them and over the ridge. The clouds broke apart, letting rays of sunlight pierce down through the gray, turning it gold. Below them, the flood's rage diminished in force.

Elam began to shake again.

"I'll get you home," Refúgio said.

He waited patiently until Elam could rise steadily to his feet, and then helped him down the hillside, across the subsiding stream, and up the far slope.

But Refúgio stopped short of entering their yard.

"I need to go now."

"How come?" Elam asked.

"I don't want to make your father mad."

The knot in the back of Elam's mind tightened once again.

———————

That evening as Elam lay in bed, he wrestled with the idea of telling his parents what had happened. In whispers to the darkened ceiling, he practiced all the ways he might break the news. He thought if Daddy knew that Refúgio had saved him, he would soften toward their friendship.

But also playing in the background of Elam's mind, nearly drowning out his own whispered explanations, were all Daddy's arguments about the dangers of this place. His scoldings about wandering the desert alone. His lectures on making the right kind of friends. His warnings about letting the past go. Elam feared that the events of the day would be more likely to rekindle his father's anger than soothe it.

But maybe it was worth the chance.

Chapter Twenty-one

Elam awoke with bruised and aching muscles. He half fancied the stiffness was a result of his arguments with himself the night before. As he climbed out of bed, however, it became obvious that the flood had battered his body more than he realized. His left shoulder hurt and a large bruise discolored the back of his thigh.

He sat on the edge of his bed and glanced at the clock on his nightstand. Seven-fifteen. Daddy would already have left for work. Elam was relieved that he had until this afternoon to gather his courage. He had decided to tell his parents about yesterday, his hope winning out against his fear. But still, he needed the time to fix his mind to it.

As he sat there, holding his jeans on his lap, it seemed the stiffness of his body began to seep into his mind. He felt faded and distant, his sight focusing on a spot in the air, just off the floor. Only a disjointed echo of helplessness penetrated his thoughts—the helplessness of being swept away by the flood. A far-off part of him wondered if Brett had felt that way, too.

A tap-tapping on the window interrupted his torpor. He glanced up to see Refúgio signaling to him. Coming to himself, he pulled on his jeans and tee shirt and crossed to the window. Refúgio had disappeared.

Elam hurried outside and scanned the yard. He spotted his friend peeking in through the gate, half-hiding behind the cinder-block wall. With a glance back at the house, Elam rushed down the steps.

He opened the gate. "Come on in."

"No," Refúgio said. "You've got to come see it. What the storm did."

"What?" Elam stepped out into the dirt road. "What happened?"

"The tree. Your tree. It's . . . let's go." He pulled at Elam's arm, tugging him across the road, toward the canyon.

"Let me get some shoes first. Come on in."

Refúgio released him. "No. I'll wait here." He stopped at the edge of the road and pushed his hands into the back pockets of his pants. "But hurry."

Twenty minutes later Elam stood with Refúgio at the mouth of the basin, his heart full of lead. The pine tree lay across the sand, its bedraggled roots exposed to the air. A few dirt-caked irises were strewn across the basin's floor, but the other plants had been swept clean away.

"We've got to fix it!" Elam cried, racing to the tree. "Help me." He began pulling at it, trying to lift it upright. "Come on! Help me!"

The branches on the underside of the tree were half buried in the sand and dirt that had washed down from above, but with Refúgio's aid, Elam was able to shake the tree loose and raise it up.

With their hands they dug a new hole for it, at the side of the basin, out of the way of future flooding. They wrestled the tree into its new spot and carefully packed the dirt around its roots, tamping the soil down with their feet.

They stepped back to appraise their work. The tree leaned at an awkward angle.

"Maybe we should stake it," suggested Refúgio. He tried to push it straight.

But Elam stopped short with a sudden realization. "The spring . . . it's gone!"

The basin wall was dry.

Elam raced up the trail, angling across the slope to the right and then back up to the left, to the source of the spring. He could hear Refúgio panting behind him. The sand had been sculpted smooth, erasing all evidence that water had once bubbled up from the ground there—except for a dampness that took refuge in the thin sliver of shade at the foot of the step.

Refúgio slumped down on the ground and let out a sigh. "The magic is gone," he said.

"We'll just have to bring water from home," Elam said, wiping the sweat off his face. "We'll just have to make sure the tree gets watered."

Refúgio waited on the dirt road while Elam filled the first bucket. Then they took turns carrying it down into the canyon and up the gully under the blazing midday sun, stopping occasionally to snatch a drink for themselves. Once the pine was well watered, they found an old metal fence post behind the Richardses' house and pounded it deep into the ground beside the tree. With a length of clothesline from Elam's back yard they pulled the trunk straight and anchored it to the fence post.

"That should hold it," Elam said.

Refúgio nodded. He stripped off his shirt and wiped his face with it. "For now at least."

Elam dropped his hammer into the bucket. "We can bring more water in the morning." He scanned the afternoon sky. "If only this place would stay shaded more."

"Maybe it'll rain," suggested Refúgio.

"No! I'll just water it myself." Elam snatched up the bucket.

On their way back to Elam's house, Refúgio stopped at the canyon's floor. "I ought to go now." He turned down the wash.

"Where?"

Refúgio paused. "Home."

"I'll go with you," Elam said.

"No, that's all right."

Refúgio jogged off, leaving Elam to stand alone under the late afternoon sun. Elam watched him disappear around a bend. Suddenly Elam panicked, afraid that Refúgio would somehow slip away. He dropped the bucket and raced after him, keeping to the edges of the wash, scurrying along, trying to keep Refúgio in sight, but careful not to be seen himself.

Refúgio loped past the end of the ridge of houses and came to the highway that led out of town. Twin culverts tunneled under the shimmering blacktop. Refúgio climbed onto the road and vanished down the far side. The culverts were clogged with tumbleweeds and other debris that had swept down the canyon during past thunderstorms. Elam peered into their lengths of darkness, then crept up onto the road himself.

He followed on through the desert, far enough behind that the noise of Refúgio's steps was swallowed up in the eerie silence. As he hurried along, Elam felt as if he were in turn being watched—his path traced by hidden eyes that peered down at him from the surrounding hills. He yearned to call out for Refúgio to wait. Instead he quietly trailed after his friend.

The wash widened, fanning out into a flat dotted with creosote and scrubby mesquite. Still Refúgio continued, and still Elam kept up his pursuit. At last Refúgio came to a dirt road—a rutted track that gouged its way through the rocks and sand, leaving scraggly plants growing up between the ruts.

Elam ducked behind a bush as Refúgio turned left to follow the track. After a moment, Elam stole onto the path himself. The sun had descended toward the hills at his back, stretching his shadow out before him. He feared it would catch up to the other boy and give away his presence, but he didn't dare lag any farther behind.

Finally the road climbed a slight rise. Refúgio crested the top and disappeared. Elam kept low and hurried upward, his breath coming in gasps. He stopped at the top.

The rutted path swung down across the hillside, leading to a set of cultivated fields. Watermelon vines sprawled over the nearer field. Beyond that grew cotton. Past the fields a row of tall, desert-bred cedar trees stood as a break in the monotony. Through the trees Elam caught a glimpse of a wide riverbed and the glint of water between rocks.

A house trailer, missing wheels and axle, sat flat on the dusty ground just before the fields, its silver finish dulled with streaks of rust. Tattered curtains hung in its windows, and an absurd metal chimney pierced its roof. Tumbleweeds had piled up against its side almost to the windows.

Refúgio disappeared around the front of the trailer.

Elam hurried down the sloping road, skipping over rocks and shabby plants. He slowed, however, as he approached the trailer. A humming sound filled the air.

Back home in the mountains, he and Brett had once come across a wild beehive just gone to swarm. The two had found delight in the sky turned dark with bees and the constant buzzing drone. The humming Elam heard now was similar, only deeper, richer.

He moved closer, listening. The sound seemed to come from the trailer itself. He crept to the near side and peeked around. At the front a veranda fashioned from saguaro ribs and ocotillo spears shaded the entrance to the battered trailer. Trumpet vines with their orange-red blossoms twined through the rough construction, covering the thorny supports with a ceiling and walls of green.

Small, opalescent shapes flitted through the greenery, darting from flower to flower—tiny birds with wings that beat so fast they were invisible.

Elam stepped under the veranda. A thrumming past his ear made him duck his head. Hundreds of miniature birds hung in the air, bobbing on hidden currents, disappearing, then reappearing, as if they had temporarily blinked out and then back into existence. Elam stood hypnotized by their flitting movements and the droning hum. It was several moments before the opening of the trailer door startled him from his reverie.

Refúgio stepped out and stopped in surprise.

"Uh, hi," Elam said, suddenly uncomfortable.

Refúgio stared at him. "You followed me."

"Yeah, I . . . I did."

"Why?"

All the reasons flooded through Elam's mind: *because I didn't want to be alone, because I didn't want to go home, because I didn't want you to get away.* He shrugged. "I just wanted to see where you lived," he said.

Refúgio frowned. "Why?"

Elam was beginning to feel embarrassed—both for himself and for Refúgio's apparent discomfort. The noise of the hummingbirds disturbed his thoughts, making him speak louder than he meant to. "Because. Because you wouldn't tell me."

"Refúgio," called a graveled voice from inside the trailer. "*¿Quién está?*"

"*No hay nadie, Papi.*" Refúgio gazed at Elam. "There is no one," he repeated.

"Who was that?" Elam asked.

"My grandfather." Refúgio let the door swing shut. "So now you know where I live, you can go home."

"But—"

"I have work to do." He bent down and pulled a large wrench from a wooden toolbox that butted up against the trailer. "Maybe your father was right. Maybe you should have your own friends." He started out from under the veranda, heading toward the fields. "Can you find your way back by yourself?"

"Yeah, but—"

"You better hurry before it gets dark."

Though Elam hurried as Refúgio suggested, the last shreds of daylight were melting into night when he climbed out of the canyon and up into his own back yard. He entered the house and found Momma sitting alone at the kitchen table.

"Where have you been?" she asked, a rare anger showing in her eyes. "You've got your father out looking for you."

Elam slumped into a chair. "What for?"

"He got worried when you didn't come home for dinner."

"What does he care?"

"Elam!"

"Well, he doesn't."

The kitchen door squeaked open behind him. Daddy stood against the darkness of the living room. He must have come in the front door just as Elam came through the back.

"I been to every house on Smelter Road," Daddy said in a quiet voice. It was the tight kind of quiet that meant Elam had better not interrupt. "I should have known you wouldn't be at any of them. You been out tramping around."

Elam tried to speak, but Daddy cut him off. "Maybe you oughta get to bed."

Elam could hear the unspoken warning. He pushed out of his chair, and without even a good-night to Momma, he headed to his room. There he pulled out the snakeskin box Refúgio had made for him. He ran his fingers over the smooth scales. Though the room was dark, he imagined he could see the box through his fingers—the tawny colors, the diamond markings. He clenched his teeth. Somehow he had to make Daddy understand. He had to convince his father that he needed Refúgio. Perhaps if Daddy knew all that Refúgio had done. . . .

He carried the box into the kitchen. Daddy sat at the table with his ever-present cup of coffee. He had been talking in low tones to Momma.

Elam set the box on the table. "Refúgio made this," he said. He kept his gaze riveted on the box, afraid that if he looked up his father would interrupt before he had a chance to finish. "He barely even knew me, and he made it for me."

He lifted the lid. "I keep all my stuff in it. Look." He picked up the .22 casing. "Remember this? You came busting out of the house like you were afraid I was dead."

He hesitated, searching for the right words. "I . . . I like Refúgio. I want him to be my friend. But now maybe it's too late." He finally glanced up to see his father's reaction.

Daddy was staring at the tabletop, running a finger around the rim of his coffee cup.

Elam closed the lid of the box and stood silently for a moment. Finally a rush of words burst from him. "Do you know how many times I see Brett every day? Do you know how many times I think,

If I'd only been there? When I'm with Refúgio I don't have to feel that way. I don't have to remember that I was the one that found Brett!" His head drooped forward. "I don't have to hear his voice. . . . "

Elam suddenly felt exhausted from the long day. "I just thought you should know." He returned to his bedroom and closed the door. Sprawled back on his bed, he wondered if his outburst had done any good. Daddy had barely even moved a finger.

Chapter Twenty-two

Elam awoke the next morning remembering something Refúgio had told him: *My grandfather says
snakes live forever.* He pulled the bedsheet up over
his shoulders. "Nothing lives forever," he muttered.
He peeked one-eyed at the bedside clock. Six-
thirty. His father would be leaving for work soon.

Elam groaned, stretched out his arms and legs,
then rolled to his side and closed his eyes.

"Son?" Daddy called with a tap on the door.
"Are you awake?"

Elam didn't answer.

"Son?" The door creaked open. "May I come in?"

Elam kept his face turned to the wall. His
father's work boots squeaked on the wooden floor.

"You left this," Daddy said.

Elam rolled over, pushing his hair out of his eyes. Daddy held out the snakeskin box.

"Thanks." Elam climbed out of bed and took the box, avoiding his father's face.

"You say Refúgio made it?" Daddy asked.

"Uh-huh."

"He does fine work."

"His grandpa taught him how." Elam placed the box in his drawer.

"Brett was a good friend," Daddy said, as if it were an idea that had just occurred to him.

Elam nodded, still staring down at the box next to his shirts.

"I thought moving away would help you get back to how you was, help you forget. Maybe making new friends . . . a new place . . . " Daddy cleared his throat. "Maybe I was wrong."

Elam looked up, but Daddy was staring out the far window, hesitating as if there were something more he wanted to say. At last he continued. "I been thinking a lot about what you said last night. Maybe I was wrong about you and that boy, too." He turned and looked at Elam. "Nobody should have to lose their best friend twice."

He pushed his hand through his hair. Then he turned to leave. "I've got to get to work now. We'll talk this evening." He pulled the door closed behind him.

Elam stared at the place his father had stood. Something had just passed between them, and he was struggling to understand what it was. *We'll talk this evening,* his father had said. And, *Maybe I was wrong.*

———————————

Elam left the house just after breakfast. He had hoped to find Refúgio waiting in the road, waiting to help carry today's bucket of water to the pine tree. But the road was empty. He would have to manage on his own.

He poured out the first bucket at the base of the ragged tree, then slumped down to the sand.

He looked up at the brittle branches and drying needles. "Nothing lives forever," he said, remembering Refúgio's words. He wished Refúgio were there. He wanted to rehearse with him all he might say to his father this evening. He wanted to tell them both about Brett. About growing up together. About sleeping under the stars and not being afraid because they had each other's company. About secrets they shared and quarrels that neither ever won.

Most of all, Elam wanted to talk about being torn into little pieces when he found Brett's body, wedged between two boulders a hundred yards downstream from where he was supposed to have been fishing. Elam wanted to ask how he could ever feel whole again.

But Refúgio wasn't there.

Elam buried his face in his arms.

The piercing whistle from the smelter startled him. Three short blasts sounded, echoing off the hillsides.

Elam jumped up. It was too early for shift change—not even noon yet. He wondered what it meant. The whistle sounded again, repeating the same pattern of three. Curious, he headed back down the gully. The whistle continued, three blasts followed by a short pause, over and over.

Elam hurried, each cycle of the signal making him more anxious.

When he reached the wash, he peered apprehensively in the direction of the smelter.

"Something's happened up there," a voice said.

Elam spun about.

Dicky and Mike trudged toward him in the sand.

"Yeah, a fire or something," Dicky said.

"A fire?" asked Elam.

Mike shielded his eyes with one hand. "That's the fire alarm." He swatted at Dicky's shoulder. "Let's go see." He turned to Elam. "You wanna come?"

Elam felt a sudden tightening in the pit of his stomach. "A fire at the smelter?"

"Could be," said Dicky.

"Or anywhere in town," added Mike. "The copper company runs *all* the emergency crews."

Though Elam tried to feel relief that his father was not in danger, the knot remained in his stomach.

"Come on," said Mike.

With a nervous curiosity, Elam followed the two boys. At the far curve of the canyon they came to a chain-link fence that stretched down one side and up the other, marking the smelter's property. Mike lay on his back in the sand and pulled himself under the fence.

"Is it—is it all right to go in?" Elam asked.

"Yeah," said Dicky. "The fence is just to keep animals out." He dropped to his belly and crawled after Mike.

"Hurry up," Mike said. He pulled on the fence, giving Elam more space to wriggle through.

The alarm grew louder as they angled up the hill and into a gravel parking lot. Dicky and Mike ducked behind a car. Elam knelt beside them. His heart seemed to be pounding in time to the whistle blasts. He peered around the side of the car at the gateway into the smelter proper.

A white station wagon raced into the parking lot, stirring up a cloud of dust. It skidded to a halt before the gate.

"Somebody must be hurt," Mike said. "That's the ambulance."

To Elam it was like watching the scene from a distance—from outside himself. Two men jumped from the station wagon and raced to meet a couple of workers who had appeared from inside the plant. The four disappeared through the gateway.

For no accountable reason Elam felt shaky in his arms and legs. He noticed how hot it had gotten in the dusty parking lot. There was no shade, and the cars seemed to give off a heat of their own.

The alarm stopped.

Dicky and Mike sneaked toward the gate, scurrying from car to car. Elam stayed behind. He felt guilty for intruding in a place where he had no business.

He heard the crunch of gravel as another car pulled into the lot. He watched it roll to a stop beside the ambulance. The doors opened with a heavy *chunk* and slammed shut again.

Elam didn't recognize the man who drove the car, but he knew the woman who had exited on the passenger's side.

"Isn't that your mom?" Mike asked. He had appeared out of nowhere.

"Uh, yeah," Elam answered, half in a daze.

"What's she doin' here?"

"I . . . I don't know."

Momma paced before the gate as if she was waiting for something. Elam jumped from his hiding place and raced toward her.

"Momma," he cried.

She turned, searching the parking lot. When she spied him, she ran forward and grabbed him in her arms. "Oh, Elam."

———— — ————

Daddy was dead. That's what they said. A crane had collapsed on him, crushing his chest under a half-ton of steel. That's what they said. They said it was quick, that he hadn't felt a thing. But the only part Elam understood for sure was that Daddy was dead.

Strange voices filled the house that evening. People Elam had never met sat on the couch in the small living room. Men and women came and went, visiting quietly with one another while Momma sat at the table in the kitchen, Mrs. Gardner at her side.

Elam kept to his room. He tried to remember the words of that morning's conversation. He tried in vain to remember what Daddy had looked like, what he had said.

But it was no use. It was as if his mind was frozen.

Chapter Twenty-three

As Elam tried to sleep that night, the August heat crawled over his skin, making him toss and turn in discomfort. He had kept the light on for company, but that seemed to make the night stretch on forever. The last he remembered, his bedside clock was stuck on two. When he rolled awake sometime later, the light had been turned off, leaving the room in darkness. A hot breeze whispered through the open window.

He dozed again and awoke to early daylight. He dragged out of bed with his eyes smarting and a dull pain in the middle of his forehead. He pushed at it, trying to ignore its source. *It didn't happen,* a voice in the back of his mind said.

He shuffled out of his room, wanting to believe the voice.

Momma sat at the kitchen table, still in the clothes she had worn the day before. Her face was dry and rigid like clay.

"Are we going home now?" Elam asked. His voice sounded distant to his own ears.

She looked at him as if he were a stranger.

"I'll start packing," he said.

He returned to his room, gathered up the dirty clothes he had thrown into the corner, and shoved them into a drawer. Then he went out to the cellar, where the cardboard boxes had been stowed from their move. He figured three would be enough.

Concentrating on the task at hand, he emptied his closet into the boxes. Finally all that remained was the box he had left packed nearly the whole summer ago. He slid it out into the center of the room and pulled it open. It contained old photographs and other odds and ends.

He lifted out a picture. It had been taken when he was five or six. In it he stood alongside Daddy — his fishing partner before Brett — holding up a string of trout they had caught at Big Lake. He pulled out another photo. He was eight, sitting on the hood of the pickup with Daddy grinning behind the steering wheel. In the next one he was four, perched on Daddy's shoulders. Another. And another. He dropped each one into his lap. They began to blur, their blacks and whites running into a glimmering pile of old memories.

He jumped up and the photographs scattered across the floor. Hardly knowing where he was headed, he raced out of the house. There was too much in his head.

As he stumbled off the back porch, the sun burned the tears from his eyes. He caught himself and stopped, not ten feet from the rattlesnake coiled in the middle of the cement walk. It must have crawled up into the yard to bask in the morning warmth. Its audacity offended him. He backed away, his fists clenched. He hurried to the tool shed, just by the cellar door, and grabbed a shovel. It's what Daddy would have done. But Daddy was gone, and so it was Elam who had to protect Momma now. Like everything else in this inhospitable country, the rattler was a danger.

Elam raised the shovel and took careful aim. If he missed he might not have another chance—the snake would fight back, striking with poisoned fangs, its rattle buzzing with alarm. Elam had to stop that alarm from sounding.

But before he could swing the shovel, a mourning dove cried out its throaty *croo-croo* from within the branches of the cottonwood tree. And though it was full daylight, with the sun already risen from the hills, the call of a lone coyote echoed through the air.

Elam stood frozen with the shovel clutched in his hands—the shovel he and Refúgio had used to bury another coyote so many days before. The shovel he had used to plant impossible irises around the makeshift grave.

The snake, too, remained still, ignoring its own danger. Elam lowered the shovel, then sank to the ground. His face streamed with tears that now even the desert sun could not steal away.

Oblivious to everything around him, Elam sobbed, uncontrollable with grief. Confused by the enormity of his pain, he tried to keep his mind fixed on the memory of the coyote, the poor animal lying lifeless in the wash. Killed when it might have been saved.

As Elam hiccuped for breath, he felt a comforting weight slide over his legs. Startled, he looked up through tear-blurred eyes. The diamondback slithered away across the sparse grass. With a flick of its tail, it disappeared beneath the cottonwood tree.

Elam could still feel the touch on his legs. He rose to his feet. He wiped his eyes and breathed a deep, shuddering sigh. He looked into the sun that had risen over the hills. It burned the clouds out of the sky, melting them into the high and distant blue.

A hot breeze pushed at him from behind, curling around him, winding across his shoulders and through his legs. It tugged at him, and he followed. It pulled him on into the canyon, stirring up miniature dust devils in its passing.

The sun rose overhead in a rapid arc toward noon. The shadows on the hillside shrank as if the heat were too much for them. It seemed as if the whole morning sped by in the time it took Elam to climb up into the sheltered alcove, both time and he pushed along by an unseen hand.

The pine tree stood as he had last left it, supported by a rusting fence post and a length of clothesline. Dry needles formed a brittle carpet around its trunk.

Nothing lives forever.

It was like an echo of his own voice, still lingering from what seemed ages ago, before his world had come crashing down with the collapse of a crane. But perhaps the echo was wrong? Elam slowly approached the tree, his mouth open in surprise. The luminescent green of new growth sprouted from the tip of each branch.

―――――

It was full noon by the time Elam drifted home. He pulled open the screen door and felt like he had stepped back through time. Momma still sat at the kitchen table. It seemed as if she hadn't stirred from that spot since he'd left early in the morning.

"Momma?" he said. "I'm home."

It was then he realized she wasn't alone. Mrs. Gardner was at the counter, pouring a mug of coffee from the blue-and-white–speckled pot. "Hello, Elam," she said as she stirred sugar into the steaming cup. "How are you doing?" She placed the mug on the table before his mother, then sat down next to her.

"I'm okay," he said.

"Where you been?" Momma asked, her voice touched with impatience.

"Just out walking."

"You know your father didn't like you going off alone."

Elam nodded. "I know."

Momma leaned on her hands, her palms pushed against her eyes. Somehow it changed her voice, made it seem to come from far away.

"Why'd we ever have to come here?" she asked.

Elam hesitated, wondering if the question was meant for him.

Mrs. Gardner touched her shoulder. "Helen, it'll just make you go crazy thinking things like that."

"I can't help it. I can't help but think if we'd done things different . . . " Her lip trembled and she turned away.

Elam's heart felt like it was being torn in two. He was the reason they had come here. It was his fault. He could feel it in Momma's words as he fled to his room.

***

A long afternoon later, Elam squatted just on the rise of a dirt road and stared down the slope at a dilapidated trailer. Despite the warmth, a faint wisp of smoke rose from its chimney. From beyond the trailer, out near the fields, came the putting drone of a gasoline engine that pumped water from a deep well to irrigate the watermelon and cotton. Elam watched, hidden atop the hill, while Refúgio went about his work, controlling the irrigation, channeling the water into each row with the turn of a shovel.

Elam wanted to call out, to run straight down the hillside and tell Refúgio about the pine tree, how they had saved it. Instead he watched motionless while Refúgio switched off the pump, kicked the dirt from his cowboy boots, and disappeared into the trailer to leave the fading afternoon in silence.

Elam could tell by the length of his own shadow that the sun had begun to set at his back. He should be heading home soon, but still he sat and stared at the trailer, trying to peer through its thin walls.

Momma had said that Uncle Jack was coming. He was probably already at the house. Elam couldn't bring himself to face anyone. If he had handled Brett's death better, Daddy might still be alive. Or better yet, if Brett had never died . . .

Elam pulled at a spiny weed that grew at the side of the road. He examined the uprooted plant in the fading light. Brett's death was his fault, too. If only he'd been there like they planned, instead of arriving too late.

———————

A velvet rim surrounded the world when Elam finally pushed himself to his feet. The fire in the west had faded and a few stars were already glimmering in the deep blue sky. As he walked along through the growing dusk, the familiar cry of a coyote sounded from off to his left. It was echoed by another from the hills on the right—a mournful cry that Elam ached to answer. But he didn't know how.

He continued on across the desert. The coyotes' subdued cries were joined by other whining barks. Soon the whole pack seemed to be following along with him, keeping themselves at a bearable distance. Their presence offered a strange kind of comfort.

Elam crossed the highway into the canyon. Four-legged shadows flitted across the blacktop like phantoms on either side. They turned quiet. The rising moon dusted the landscape with a ghostly frost. The stars grew brighter. The night sky turned both deep and close, touchable and infinite. The illusion made Elam dizzy, as if his attachment to the ground had grown uncertain.

He hurried up the hillside and left behind the company of the sympathetic animals. As he suspected, Uncle Jack was already at the house, waiting with Momma in the kitchen. He was a big man, taller and broader than Daddy. But softer, too. Elam remembered that when he spied him leaning back against the kitchen counter, rolling a battered cowboy hat in his hands.

Momma had been pacing the floor. Elam could tell by how she turned when he came in. And she was angry. "Elam! Don't I have enough to worry about without you constantly running off?"

But Uncle Jack wrapped his arm around Elam and pulled him close. "Helen, go easy on the boy. He's just lost his father."

Elam buried his face in the tobacco smell of Uncle Jack's shirt. Though he tried to stop them, the tears welled up from deep inside and came pouring out once again. Uncle Jack's sympathy was too much to bear.

After a late dinner, the three of them sat quiet around the kitchen table. Uncle Jack tried to start

up conversation, asking unimportant questions that
Momma answered with token words.

At last Elam excused himself. He retired to his
dark room and sat on the edge of his bed. The coyotes had started up again, calling to one another
across the distance. He remembered what Refúgio
had told him—that they howled because they didn't
like the empty night. Somehow their cries touched
the emptiness he felt inside. But they couldn't fill it.
He doubted anything in this barren desert could.

Chapter Twenty-four

One more day in this place. One more day of unbearable heat. One more day of longing for home. Tomorrow they would be taking Daddy back to Springerville to lay him to rest. Today Elam would keep to his room. Momma and Uncle Jack had enough to worry about making preparations. They didn't need to fret over him, too. So he stayed inside, out of the way, quiet and inconspicuous.

Round about midmorning he heard a knock at the back door. Uncle Jack's voice rumbled through the house as he spoke to whoever was there. After a moment he peeked into Elam's room.

"Someone here to see you," he said.

To Elam's surprise Refúgio stood on the back porch, peering in through the screen.

Elam pulled the door open. "Hello," he said.

"Hello."

"You wanna come in?"

"No. I've got to get back home soon. I just . . . "
Refúgio glanced down at his feet. "I heard about
your father." He rushed through the words, as if in a
hurry to get them all said. "I heard about the acci-
dent. I had to come and tell you, I hope everything
will be all right. I just wanted to let you know,
I'm . . . I'm sorry."

Elam nodded. He wanted to say he was sorry,
too. He wanted to explain about the other day,
about following Refúgio home. He wanted to talk
until there was nothing left to say. Instead he just
held the screen door open, nodding like he understood.

"Well, I've got to go now," Refúgio said. *"Adiós."*

"Bye." Elam let the door swing closed. Now it
was his turn to watch through the screen while
Refúgio hurried away. After a moment, Elam
pushed the door open again and followed, wondering why he could never say what he felt.

As he stepped once more into the canyon, sibilant whispers murmured on all sides, rising up with
waves of morning heat. Dry air crackled over his
face. Refúgio had already disappeared beyond the
curve of the slope, but still Elam did not feel
alone—the desert itself surrounded him now, a living presence that pulled at him, more insistent than

ever. He eased downward, and it was like descending into a dream.

Shimmers of warmth flowed along the wash, forming an indistinct river. Elam waded through its current. He could feel it tugging at his legs. He passed on through, drawn again up the gully to the pine tree. The green had spread along each branch, and now the tree stood full and vibrant against the gray backdrop. It was not possible. Or it was a dream.

"Or magic," Elam said aloud.

The soft whispers continued around him — soothing whispers that carried echoed words.

Mmmmagic . . .

"Just like Refúgio said."

Refúgio ssssaid . . .

He ran his fingers over the surface of the rock wall. Moisture began to trickle from above, coating the wall with a crystal sheen. Yellow mosses and lichens sprouted under his touch. A rushing sound like a breeze among aspens swirled about him. He spun around. Green shoots sprang up to carpet the floor of the basin. A second pine sapling poked its way through the new growth. And then another, unfurling its tiny branches to reach out for the warm sunlight.

Elam felt like laughing out loud.

"It's not dead," he cried. "It's all real!"

. . . real . . . came the echo.

Yesterday, the rattlesnake and the coyotes brought him comfort. Now the desert itself offered him a homecoming. With arms spread wide, Elam accepted the gift.

He clambered back down the gully, excited. The trickling water flowed after him, growing into a tumbling stream, filling the air with chattering conversation. At his passing, wildflowers blossomed on the banks—snowdrops and columbine, paintbrushes, wild strawberry, and bright yellow sunflowers.

He breathed in the sweetness of the new blossoms. He could feel the desert retreating from the burgeoning advance—giving way to the riot of impossible growth that followed him down the hillside. Sumac and chokecherry; towering ponderosa pines thick with long-fingered needles and stubby cones; thistles and ferns; moss and lichens and mushrooms the size of cracker boxes—all joined together to obscure the raw scarcity of this place.

In an instant the last three months sloughed away, and Elam *was* home. Breezes moved through the trees in natural rhythms, whispering, but with no will of their own. He breathed in the smells of damp earth and pine-scented air. He felt a power returning to him, a swelling within as he swept through the undergrowth, trampling a path through the alpine greenery.

The exhilaration exhausted him. He sank to the ground and was nearly swallowed by the cushion of soft vegetation. Sunlight filtered through the trees. He blinked his eyes closed and lay motionless, basking in the comfort of sifting breezes and dappled light. A voice called to him.

Elam. I'm here.

He looked up to see a figure outlined by the radiance—a towheaded boy standing with arms akimbo. Elam knew the figure couldn't be real. But there he was with blue sky and pine boughs at his back.

"It's good to see you again," he whispered. He swung his arms out, enjoying the cool touch of new greenery. Still on his back, he reached high over his head to stretch a year's worth of pain from his body.

"Ouch!" he cried.

Something had pricked his arm.

He rolled to his stomach and hunted through the clustered plants behind him. Carefully he pulled aside the ferns and creeping vines and uncovered a helmet-shaped pincushion—a miniature cactus that bristled from beneath the choking greenery. A small, white blossom adorned its crown, struggling in a feeble attempt to spread its petals.

Elam's heart began to break all over again. Through blurred eyes, he tried to focus on the tiny cactus. He brushed his fingers over the fishhook thorns. It would suffocate if he didn't do something. He tugged at the other plants, uprooting them, frantically pushing them back to make room for the cactus. Finally free, its flower stretched upward toward the sun.

Elam blinked against the tears. He unwound a creeper from the thorns. "You don't have to do this," he said. "Not for me." He pushed himself to his feet. "Please, you don't have to do this."

The scene about him seemed to freeze expectantly, as if unsure of his words. The breeze died, the air became still.

Elam rubbed the scratch on his arm. "I'll be all right."

The tallest trees wavered, as if seen through water. And then a sound, like a sigh of relief, whooshed through the air. Elam felt a sudden warmth on the back of his neck. The forest began to evaporate in the blazing light, melting into tattered shreds of greenery.

He shielded his eyes. "But thank you," he cried to whatever would hear.

The answering warmth sank through his shoulders and into his chest. He sighed, too. "Thank you," he whispered.

With just a trace of mountain air lingering at his back, he picked a path down the hillside, stepping carefully through the scattered cholla cactus and prickly pear. But he didn't go home just yet. There was something he had to do.

The drone of the hummingbirds formed a pleasant background noise to Elam's rap on the trailer's screen door. When Refúgio answered, Elam gestured toward the birds. "How do you get them to stay?" he asked.

"They like the flowers," Refúgio said. Then he pushed the screen open and stepped outside.

A hummingbird darted between them and disappeared beyond the veranda.

"I followed you again," Elam said.

Refúgio nodded.

Now it was Elam who rushed through the words. "I have to tell you something. About the other day. I followed you because I was afraid you were going away. That I wouldn't see you again. Because . . . because I didn't want to be alone. I didn't mean to spy. I'm sorry."

Refúgio started to speak, but Elam continued. "I told you my best friend died. I didn't have any other friends until I met you." He looked down. "I think because you're different. You don't remind me of

Brett, like everyone else did—not the same way at least."

"Because I'm not a gringo?" Refúgio asked.

"I think so, at first. But I was wrong. So was my father. He told me, just before . . . he told me that morning. He told me he was wrong, too. He said I shouldn't lose my best friend twice. He meant you."

Elam looked into Refúgio's eyes. "You never asked me about Brett, about what happened. You asked about *me.* Everybody else wanted to know how Brett died, what he looked like when I found him. Everybody else just made me remember. You didn't."

He fell silent. With relief, he realized he had said the words. He had told Refúgio the truth.

"I'll understand if you hate me," he added. "But I hope you don't."

He waited for a response.

Refúgio turned and called back inside the trailer, speaking words in Spanish that Elam could not understand.

"*Sí, está bien,*" came the reply from the darkness.

Refúgio returned Elam's gaze. "I'll take you home, if you want."

———

When Elam and Refúgio arrived at the house, Momma was at the kitchen table with Uncle Jack. The two sat across from a man in a dark suit who was filling out papers and asking for Momma's signature here and there.

Momma looked up at Elam in relief. "There you are," she said. She smiled for the first time in what seemed forever. She turned to Refúgio. "Thank you for bringing my son home. Please, stay to lunch."

Refúgio nodded.

Uncle Jack stood up and stretched. "Everything's been taken care of," he said. "We'll lay your daddy to rest at Flag Hollow, next to your grandma." He put his hand on Elam's shoulder. "It'll take some time, but you and your momma will be all right. We'll all take care of you." He wiped his face with a handkerchief. "It's hotter than blazes here. I reckon you'll be happy to be moving back home."

Elam glanced at Refúgio. "I reckon," he said.

Momma didn't say anything.

───────────────

That night Elam went to bed accompanied by coyote yipping and moaning. The desert hillsides were again full of their mournful cries. He slipped out from under the sheets and padded to Momma's room.

She stirred when he opened the door. "Can't you sleep either?" she asked.

Elam crossed the moonlit floor and sat on the edge of her bed.

"I've been thinking."

"About what?"

"About Brett and Daddy."

Momma pushed herself up in the bed. "Honey, you mustn't worry yourself too much."

"No, it's not that. I realized something is all."

"What's that?"

"Well, you remember how the day Brett died, I was supposed to go with him, but I was late."

"I know, son. You can't blame yourself."

"It's not that neither—though I did blame myself. Until today. I learned something. You know why I was late?"

Elam could see Momma shake her head in the pale light.

"I remembered it was because Daddy made me stay behind and clean out the toolshed. By the time I was done, it was *too* late. And then when I found him, Momma, it crushed me inside, and I had to blame myself. I had to, because he was my best friend. If I couldn't save him, who could? If I'd only been there. Then today I remembered—"

"Elam, you can't blame your daddy neither."

"I know that, too. Brett did what he decided to do, what he wanted to do. Just like Daddy deciding to move us here. That wasn't my fault neither."

Momma was quiet. She reached out and took Elam's hand. "I'm sorry if I made you feel that way," she said. "I didn't mean to. I wasn't myself."

"I know, Momma. It's going to be a long time 'til we feel much like ourselves. You and me, we're going to cry a lot. But I figured out today that I can't run away from it or hide it or make it go away. It'll just have to be there for a while, sort of filling in the part that's gone. Then someday we'll feel a little better."

Momma pulled him close. "Elam, how'd you get to be so smart?"

He looked out her window at the night sky. Stars glimmered around the cottonwood tree. He could still hear the coyote wails. "I had some help," he said.

Chapter Twenty-five

The next day Elam sat out on the front steps, waiting for Momma and Uncle Jack. It had been too stifling inside. Daddy never had fixed the swamp cooler. So Elam came out to the porch to wait until it was time to take Daddy back home.

He spit on the sidewalk and watched his saliva dance and sizzle on the hot surface. He could almost see Daddy standing there with a grin on his face. "By August I bet it evaporates before it even hits the ground," Daddy had said.

Elam shook his head. "You were wrong," he whispered. "It doesn't."

He looked up at the squeak of the gate. Mike Richards trudged up the steps and along the front walk.

"Where's Dicky?" Elam asked.

"Aw, he's a pest. I think he's out chasing coyotes. I don't think he ever forgave you guys for spoiling his plans." Mike chuckled. Then he turned sober. He shuffled from one foot to the other. He cleared his throat. "I'm real sorry about your dad," he finally said. "It must be tough."

Elam nodded, squinting in the bright August sun. "Thanks."

Mike sat down on the step next to Elam. "So, you'll be moving now?"

"Yeah, I guess."

"That's too bad. We could have had some fun."

Elam shrugged. "It's too hot here."

"Yeah, it is. Watch this."

Mike spit at the concrete, just like Elam had. The moisture seemed to be sucked right into the air without even dampening the walk.

Elam stared at the cement. "We . . . we're going to be leaving soon," he said.

"Oh. Will you be coming back?"

"To get our stuff, I guess. To move it back home, though I don't know where we'll live. We won't be able to afford the old house. Uncle Jack says there's a small place close to his, and Momma talked about getting a job, but there's not much work around Springerville. Unless she wants to be a cowboy."

Mike chuckled again. "Maybe you should just stay here."

"Yeah, maybe we should."

Mike stood up. "Well, good luck. I really am sorry about your dad." He walked away and out the gate.

"That's okay," Elam called after him, suddenly wishing that he could talk to Mike for just a moment longer.

Chapter Twenty-six

It was in the car, winding down through the corrugated hills toward Copperton, that Momma spoke of plans for the future. Elam sat in the front seat, staring out the window at the slow transition from piñon pine to century plants to towering saguaros. He and his mother had been mostly quiet since leaving Springerville several hours before. As the desert became more prevalent on either side of the road, the feeling that Elam was returning to a place that held attachments grew stronger. It felt like having a home to go to and a home to leave behind. But Elam knew that he really had no choice in the matter. He and Momma were only on their way back to the desert—to the house on the point—to collect all their belongings and move them back to the mountains.

Elam figured Uncle Jack would be coming down in the next few days to help them move.

Momma cleared her throat like she wanted to say something. He looked at her expectantly.

"Elam, they'll let us stay in the house, rent free, for as long as we want," she said.

He slid around in his seat. She cast him a quick glance, then turned back to face the road.

"And they'll give me a job."

Elam tried to puzzle out what Momma was saying. "Who will?"

"The copper company. Because of what happened to Daddy, they'll take care of us. If we want. I know you don't like it there, but . . . " Her voice trailed off. And then she began again. "Rhea Gardner said her husband could help us out around the house. We'll go back to Springerville often. I promise. And Uncle Jack said you can spend next summer with him, if you like. Maybe do some fishing." She grew quiet again and fixed her attention back on the winding road.

Elam looked out the window as they passed a hillside covered with bristling cholla cactus. He tried to imagine what might be on the other side of the hill. And he was pleased that Momma's news felt comfortable bouncing around inside him.

When they pulled up to the house, Refúgio was sitting on the front steps. Elam jumped out of the car and ran up through the gate. "How long have you been waiting here?" he asked.

"Elam," Momma called. "Come get your things."

"About an hour is all," Refúgio answered, standing up and stretching. "I asked your neighbor lady when you were coming. She told me you'd be here today."

"Mrs. Gardner? Yeah, my mom called her last night from up at home."

"Elam," Momma repeated. "I don't want you running off and leaving all this for me."

"All right," he called back. "I'm coming."

Refúgio followed him to the car.

Elam stopped with a hand on the gate. "We're going to be staying here," he said. "At least for a while."

"I know," Refúgio said. "Mrs. Gardner told me. And that's good, because your tree is not doing so well."

"It's still there?" Elam asked in surprise. "The pine tree? It's still there?" He figured it had disappeared with all the rest.

"Of course," Refúgio answered. "Where would it go?"

Once the car was unloaded and Elam's suitcase lay empty on his bed, Elam and Refúgio headed out the back door. As they left the yard they saw Mike Richards walking toward them on the road, scuffling his feet in the dirt, stirring up clouds of dust.

Mike broke into a grin when he saw them.

"I hear you're staying," he said to Elam as he sauntered nearer.

"Who told you?" Elam asked.

Mike nodded at Refúgio. "He did. I saw him sittin' on your porch like he was guarding the house."

Elam smiled. "Yeah, we're staying. I guess I'll be living here for a while."

"That's good," Mike said.

Elam nodded. And then he asked, "Do you have any buckets at home?"

Mike shrugged. "Sure. What for?"

Elam threw his arms over Mike's and Refúgio's shoulders. "We've got a tree that needs watering. We sure could use your help."

Chapter Twenty-seven

September had begun. School would be starting
soon. Elam and Momma had come up to the mountains for a weekend visit. Early that Saturday morning, with a lunch stowed away in his knapsack,
Elam headed to the pine-forested hills. He paused
at Flag Hollow on his way out of town. He went
first to Brett's grave, where he pulled an object out
of his knapsack. An old cigar box wrapped in a
newly shed snakeskin.

He removed a pencil-drawn map from the box
and placed it on the gravestone. "I won't be needing
this," he whispered. "We're staying in the desert.
It'll cool down there a bit in the winter." Then he
held up the empty .22 casing. "Remember this?" he
said. "I'll keep it." He shoved it in his pocket.

He crossed to another grave, back against the far

fence. The earth there was still bare from the digging, the headstone clean and unweathered. "This is for you," he said, setting the snakeskin box down on the stone. "I made it myself. Refúgio showed me how."

Elam stood for the longest time, running his finger along the lid of the box. At last he rubbed his eyes with the back of his hand. "You were right," he said. "The change did do me some good after all."

He turned and looked up at the sky. High, wispy clouds feathered against the light blue of late summer. He wished he could have brought Refúgio and Mike with him. Today was too beautiful to be alone.

He found his fishing pole right where he had left it, hidden behind the ponderosa pine alongside the river. He collected the pole and climbed Mount Baldy once again. He stood at the summit, this time greeting each familiar site with a nod of recognition.

When he completed the circle, he stopped in amazement, his attention drawn to the ground at his feet. There, sprouting up from a crack in the mountain rock, was a tiny cactus, bristling with hooked spines.

Elam laughed out loud at the misplaced plant. It bravely stood amongst the moss and lichens of the rocky summit. He bent down to touch its rigid needles.

"You're a long way from home," he said.